RUNAWAY TRAIN

Simon Doyle
RUNAWAY TRAIN

SD Press
A division of Nightsgale Books

1 3 5 7 9 10 8 6 4 2

First published in 2022 by
SD Press, a division of Nightsgale Books,
Suite 97320, PO Box 1213, Belfast, BT1 9JY

Paperback ISBN 978 1 7397276 1 1
Hardcover ISBN 978 1 7397276 0 4

Cover by SD Press

A CIP catalogue record of this book
is available from the British Library and the
Library of Trinity College Dublin

Typeset in Caslon Pro by SD Press

For Lucas.

1.

DENIS

D enis Murphy didn't wake up that morning wanting to end his life. That came later.

When the alarm on his phone tore him from sleep, he rolled over, smacked the phone into silence, and smiled. It was three days before Christmas and his old bed in Clannon Village was as good as a warm hug. His mum had cooked his favourite meal last night and his sister, Caroline, stayed home instead of working her shift at the local supermarket. It was like old times before he'd gone off to university in Dublin and forgotten what family comfort was like.

Mum was smiling, which was a rare sight.

Suicide wasn't on his mind when she gave him one of his Christmas presents early, a black hoodie with the price tag ripped off and twenty Euros stuffed in the front pocket. "In case you want to go out with your friends tonight. First round's on me."

He pulled it on and kissed her cheek as she flipped the hood over his head with a laugh.

Throwing himself into Broad Meadow River—just like his dad had done eleven years ago—was the furthest thing from his mind while Caroline conjugated her Spanish verbs in advance of her mock Junior Cert exam in the new year. "*Yo estoy, tú estás, ella está.*"

But then Mum asked that question over dinner, the one she asked every time they spoke on the phone, without fail, like an advertising jingle on a loop. "Have you met a nice girl yet?"

"Not yet," he used to say. "There's no one fit enough at uni," he'd tell her with a smile in his voice so that she'd hear how jovial he was being about it.

Caroline coughed—because she knew—and hid her face with her glass of fruit juice. And her eyes blinked a Morse-code reminder that Mum wasn't ready for the truth yet, in time with the blinking of the Christmas lights in the window.

But Denis couldn't lie anymore. Not that he was dating anybody right now, but he was sick of hiding who he was. Everyone else knew—Caroline, his friends at UCD, and the grave of his father where he once left a letter for him and then went back an hour later and burned it in case Mum found it.

Caroline was the only one he never told; she just

seemed to know.

"How many gays does it take to screw in a light bulb?" she asked him once, a couple of years ago.

He didn't dare answer, and so he looked up from his book as she stood in his bedroom doorway with a massive grin on her face. She radiated childish innocence.

"Go away."

"How many?"

"How many what?"

"How many gays does it take to screw in a light bulb?"

"I don't want to know." But he did.

"Just one," she said. And then she walked away.

"That's not even funny," Denis called after her.

When she poked her head back around the frame of his door, she added, "But it takes an entire A&E department to remove it."

He had thrown his book at the empty doorway in her wake and tried not to laugh when she shouted, "I'm not picking that up, Butt Bandit."

So, that was that. Caroline had invited herself into his confidence and sworn never to tell a soul without ever saying the words out loud.

And here was Mum with her eyes fixed on Denis, one eyebrow curled into a question mark, as her fork rained garden peas onto her mashed potato and the weatherman on the TV behind her said, "I wouldn't be expecting a white Christmas if I were you."

The smile on her lips faltered before Denis even spoke. He took a gulp of wine to moisten his dried mouth, and he said the words he'd wanted to say for more than four years. "I think I'm gay, Mum."

She placed her fork on the table beside her plate. When she stood up, the chair scraped a chill across the mottled linoleum that was worn thin in uneven patches.

"Mum?"

She picked up her plate. And she threw it against the wall.

It lay in pieces on the floor next to Denis' heart.

Only when her hands were empty did she scream.

"He's only joking, Mum."

"Jesus, Mary and Joseph. You think you're *what*?"

"Mum."

"Get out."

"Mum."

"Mammy, please. He's not serious."

She leaned forward, her knuckles tense enough to bore grooves in the tabletop, and her face was white. Her jaw muscles were taut. "You better not be serious. May God forgive your lying soul."

"Mammy," Denis said, and he realised as he said it that he hadn't called her Mammy in years. The truth was out. The pathetic tone of his voice said everything.

"Get out before I thump you. Jesus Christ, how will you ever get into Heaven? What kind of filth have you been introduced to in the city?"

Denis pushed his chair back from the table as she took a swing at him. He stomped up to his room, lifted his rucksack to the sound of his mother screaming and

Caroline crying, and he shoved some clothes into it—clothes that he had only just unpacked the night before.

And he came back downstairs with pleading tears in his eyes. "Mammy. Please. Can we talk about it?"

But she hit him. She hit him in the face with the back of her hand. "I brought you up as a Christian and this is how you repay me?"

"No, Mum," he said, and his voice splintered, tearing her name in two.

"Get out."

"Denny, go back upstairs," Caroline said.

"Get out."

"Mammy, please."

"Out."

And he got out. He stood on the doorstep as the automatic porchlight blinded him and then dimmed, casting him in darkness more complete than his sadness.

Mum was screaming behind the door. He could see the blur of her in the frosted glass, and Caroline trying to calm her down. And he scraped his knuckles down the brickwork just to feel something other than disparaging sorrow.

His mother shrieked through the door, "I wish you were never born." Denis saw Caroline pull her back from the glass. "I'd sooner he confessed to murder than tell me that," Mum's muffled voice said.

Denis kicked the garden gate and walked away.

He wasn't thinking about suicide as he marched up the street and around the corner, passed the park where a lone dog barked. He just couldn't get a proper hold of his breath, and the weight of the rucksack on his back, even though it only contained a few items of clothing, was crippling. His high-tops were mired in the quicksand of solitude.

"Happy Christmas," he heard someone say nearby, but he didn't raise his head. He trudged farther up the hill where the streetlamps got less frequent and the graffiti on the gable walls was cruder. The village's Christmas decorations didn't extend this far. He passed Clannon Village's only supermarket, where Caroline had been working part-time for almost six months. She was saving up for a trip to France with her Junior Cert friends when they were finished with their exams that coming summer.

Glistening frost blanched the inner edge of the pavement, and the yellow glow from the streetlamps was weak and humble.

He hadn't decided where he was going as he came around the corner at the top of Main Street and stumbled down the grass bank beside the humpback bridge and across the playing field which was dark and childless. The goalposts at either end stood like retracted staples, listing in their broken isolation.

He fought his way through the thick gorse bushes that ringed the field, and he followed the track half a kilometre downriver to the footbridge. When he stood above Broad Meadow River, watching the dark churn of its current fourteen feet below, he still wasn't considering ending his life.

He was thinking about his father, who jumped from this very spot eleven years ago and was found washed up on shore just north of Swords, two and a half kilometres southeast of here. Andrew Murphy scribbled a note on the back of an envelope, walked the half-kilometre from their home to the bridge, took his shoes off, rolled his socks into a ball, and left them there like a monument, a neat reminder of his passing.

It got that Denis forgot what his father looked like most of the time. He'd been eight when it happened. He'd blamed his mum, just as he blamed her now.

I wish you were never born.

When his hands gripped the high railing and his foot slotted into one of the open rungs of the iron siding, that was the first time he acknowledged the thought of ending it all. Her words punched around in his mind. *I wish you were never born.*

So did he.

His foot slipped in the frost and his fingers tightened on the railing.

She'll see. If he was gone, she'd be sorry. She'd lose her son as well as her husband.

He shouldn't have told her. Caroline was right; Mum wasn't ready. But it was too late. You can't go back in the closet once you've opened the doors.

It was over. She didn't want him. His own mother refused to accept him. He was adrift in a sea of pain, a world without a family.

I wish you were never born.

Dad was gone. He would have fixed everything. Mum would've listened to him.

Denis strengthened his resolve, put his foot back in the groove, and stepped up. But he thought about Caroline. She was five when she'd lost her father—too young to remember much about him but old enough to know he was never coming back. Denis had had to comfort her for months while their mother wasn't fit to do anything. Caroline crawled into bed beside him, clinging to her stuffed rabbit, and cried herself to sleep every night.

I wish you were—

"All right, Denny?"

Denis came down off the railings and he nodded, blinking away his tears. Tom McInnis was at the far side of the footbridge, coming towards him. Denis and Aaron, Tom's younger brother, were in the same class since Juniors, and Denis had been fantasising about Tom for years. He'd buy them beers when they were fifteen and let them use his PlayStation when he wasn't around.

At twenty-two, Tom was a little over six feet tall and had the chiselled good looks of a movie star and the slick, greasy image that came with his job at Al's Garage.

"All right?" Denis responded. He picked up his backpack as if he'd just stopped to tie his shoelace, not throw himself off the bridge.

"Jeez, it's cold. Where are you headed?"

"Just hanging around."

He heard the distant whistle of an old steam engine. The sound was so out of place that Denis waited to see if it would break the night again.

He watched Tom watching him.

"Shit," Tom said, "I'm going to be late." He punched Denis on the shoulder in solidarity and continued his journey over the bridge. "You coming?"

"Where?"

"Didn't you hear it? There's a luxury steam train on its way to Belfast. It's going to be full of booze and women, and when you put the two together, you know what that means."

"Tom."

"Come on, lad. You're doing nothing else, are you?"

When Denis didn't move, Tom came back.

"Oh, bollocks. Sorry, man. This is the spot where your dad—look, you've got a minute to pay your respects. I'll turn my back, so you've got privacy. But in sixty seconds, I'm dragging your ass onto a luxury train. No arguing."

The unseen steam train whined into the night with the long, high drawl of its whistle.

Denis' confusion settled into a storm in his stomach. "See you, Dad," he said, as he kissed his fingers and pressed them against the railing.

"Come on," Tom said.

They fought their way back through the bushes and ran across the field.

By the time they got to the small, squat station at the top of Main Street, the sound of the train was loud, and they could see smoke chugging into the darkness of the distance.

Denis looked around. The station was filled with well-dressed families with matching luggage and as they weaved through the crowd towards the platform—there were no ticket barriers on the northbound track—Denis considered turning around and camping out on the bridge with the memory of his father.

Tom pulled his sleeve. "This way." And the crowd pressed forward as the front of the train came into view.

"Here she comes," someone said.

Smoke swelled in the distance, and as the train screeched closer, a cheer rose across the platform.

Denis craned his neck for a better view. Rolling into the station was the most magnificent steam train he'd ever seen. It gleamed black and red, like something from a children's fairy tale. Thick grey smoke billowed around them, and the smell of burning coal swept ahead of its arrival.

The train's brakes screeched and whined as the crowd applauded. Tom whistled, putting his dirty fingers in his mouth. Denis liked that Tom didn't care about the grease from his job as a car mechanic; it added to the allure. He often imagined those oil-smeared hands touching him.

Denis watched as each carriage rolled by. The interior lights glowed like the warmth of heaven as happy faces stared out towards the crowd.

"Do you have a ticket?" Denis asked.

"Don't need one."

"We're sneaking on?"

Tom winked, and the smear of oil on his cheek glistened.

When the train came to a stop, each carriage door opened in time, rattling down the platform from front to rear. Inspectors in forest-green uniforms alighted with their ticket punchers and beckoned the new passengers forward.

The P.A. system blurted to life and a distorted voice said, "*The Duchess of Dublin* welcomes you on board. Sleeper carriages are clearly marked throughout the train. Please have your tickets ready for inspection. The forward three carriages are economy class. Please make your way to the forward carriages for passengers with a yellow ticket. The oversized luggage car, marked as Carriage M, is situated at the rear."

"Come on," Tom said, slapping Denis' back. He led him down the platform.

The crowd jostled forward, and Denis kept his head low, with his hood up. He followed Tom toward the rear of the platform behind a couple in their forties. If anyone was looking at them, they would think they were their surly teenage sons, not would-be stowaways.

At the dedicated luggage carriage, the train attendant took a woman's enormous suitcase and tried to heft it up the two narrow steps into the train. As the woman turned away, Tom jumped forward. "Let me help you with that."

He took the other side of the case and pushed as the

attendant backed into the train.

"You got it?"

"I got it," the man said.

When he turned deeper into the carriage, Tom grabbed Denis and pushed him onboard. "Quick. Get down."

Denis squatted between a large wooden crate and the train's wall, and he held his breath. He had no idea why a hundred-and-twenty-year-old steam train had pulled into Clannon Station, or why Tom felt the need to sneak on without a ticket, but the oil-stained older man was a distraction from his misery.

I wish you were never born.

Denis didn't care anymore.

When Tom hunkered into place beside him, Denis could smell the thick, cloying headiness of his aftershave.

Their legs touched. "Scooch up a bit."

He obeyed, moving back as far as he could. He was on a train to Belfast, cramped in the dark confines of a luggage carriage, and he no longer thought about what his mum wished.

Tom smiled and his breath was warm on Denis' face. "Got enough room?"

"Yeah."

Denis felt the train thrum beneath him and someone on the platform blew a whistle.

The Duchess of Dublin lurched forward.

2.

OLIVER

"Turn it off," Oliver said. He knew what the news story was about, and he didn't care for it.

"You're on the TV," Shiva screamed with that level of high-pitched excitement only a four-year-old can achieve.

He picked his niece up and swung her around. "I can't fit on the TV, silly. I'd fall off."

"Silly Billy," she said, and she repeated it until the words jumbled up and she lost the meaning.

"Why on earth did you agree to do such a stupid thing?" his sister asked. She plucked Shiva from his arms with her fingers extended—no four-year-old was going to ruin her fresh manicure.

Grace Prasad, twenty-seven, married to a tycoon

from Mumbai who spent more time abroad than in Dublin with his wife and child, was one of the people Oliver was desperate to get away from. That was why he'd agreed to do such a stupid thing.

"Ireland doesn't need a luxury steam train tying up the railway lines. How fast do those things go, anyway? Six kilometres an hour? They haven't even completed the high-speed rail they've been talking about for years."

Oliver shook his head and reached for the TV remote to turn it off.

"Wait," Grace said. "I want to see if they mention me."

They wouldn't. He knew they wouldn't. *"Twenty-five-year-old Oliver Lloyd, heir to the Isham-Lloyd fortune, pictured here with his on-again off-again boyfriend, Walter Mason, is set to cut the ribbon on Ireland's first luxury overnight train service this evening. Speculation is rife if Lloyd is presently involved with Mason or if their turbulent relationship is on another of their many hiatuses."*

"Boyfriend?" Grace scoffed. "How old is that footage?"

"At least eight months," Oliver said. Denario's, the restaurant they'd been filmed coming out of, had gone out of business in April. Oliver hadn't spoken to Walt Mason in the last three months. Their turbulent relationship, as the skinny little girl on the news called it, had been over for a long time.

That breakup put Oliver into a voluntary rehab programme for fourteen days and, during that time, he cleaned up his act. As the son of a media mogul, Oliver was awarded some privileges that, at times, kept his name out of the press—like his self-committal into a drug-and-alcohol detox programme—but the sleazeball paparazzi always had their way. When he was pictured leaving the rehab facility, fresh-faced and wearing low-key unlabelled grey jogging pants and a blue hoodie, the tabloid press decided that he was going back to Walt. Instead, Oliver Lloyd went home to his parents and waited for Walt to inform the world that they were over, in the only way Walt knew how—by being pictured at a nightclub with a blond twink.

Oliver had grown up in the arms of a nanny and when he thought back to the happiest moments of his childhood, it involved the smells associated with Amber, the foreign nanny, rather than his mother. He could recall the smell of her breath after eating pizza, and her hands when she picked him up in the evenings after she applied her night cream. He could still smell the charcoal from her fingers when she'd been at the local cemetery, doing her rubbings.

His mother? No doubt she smelled of gin. At least that's what she smelled like now as she came into the living room, glass in hand, and announced that Daddy would be late home, he's still in Paris.

"N'ollie's on the telly," Shiva said.

"Ollie," her grandmother corrected her.

"N'ollie has a better ring to it," Oliver said. "Now, can we turn the TV off, please?"

The car was picking him up at six that evening to

take him to the station. He had no idea why they needed him so early when the train wasn't leaving Dublin Connolly Station until almost eight-thirty.

They had contacted him a few months ago, not long after his stint in rehab, and asked if he'd like to cut the ribbon for the *Duchess of Dublin*, Ireland's premier overnight train service between Dublin and Belfast, connecting north to south with opulence—their words, not his. "Fourteen carriages of exquisite luxury for the discerning traveller," they said.

The train, a refitted steam engine, was to be Ireland's equivalent of the Trans-Siberian Express. Not that Ireland needed such a thing. His driver could take him to Belfast in less than three hours, and a train could get you there in two.

"How long will *The Duchess* take to reach Belfast?" he asked the girl on the phone.

"It's deliberately slow. It will take seven hours, forty minutes to get to Belfast, with two stopovers *en route*."

"Who the hell would pay for an eight-hour journey to Belfast when they could do it in two?"

"People with more money than sense," the girl said, then she cleared her throat, and he could imagine the crap-storm that she was going to endure by her bosses.

When she spoke again, her voice was tight and high. He knew as well as she did that she'd be fired when she hung up the phone. He liked to think that was the reason he said yes, so that she could save face. But the truth was, he needed a night away from his family, from his so-called friends who only wanted to be around him for his money. And from the memory of Walter Mason, who could burn in hell for all Oliver cared.

He squeezed Shiva when she leapt into his arms for a hug, and he nodded to his sister, who prised her daughter from his chest. He leaned in and kissed his mother on the cheek. "They're giving me a private carriage all to myself."

"You and your entourage," Grace said.

"Only Annabelle. I'm giving everyone else the night off. Anyway, I'll be back in the morning. Scott will pick me up from the Europa."

"Scott can't do that," Mother said. "He's taking me to Cork tomorrow morning."

"Dave, then. Or I'll drive myself if I have to. I'll buy a car in Belfast."

He left them watching the news and went to his room. Often, it was the only time his mother paid any attention to his whereabouts, by learning about it on TV.

Upstairs, he undressed and went into his private bathroom. There was no mirror in here. Since he first entered the public eye as a young teenager, he had been compared to James Dean, some dead guy he knew nothing about. But the crazy women of the world loved him and, therefore, fell in love with Oliver, too. He stopped looking at himself when his on-call hair and makeup crew became a constant at his side.

He never exactly came out. He brought a boy home one evening when he was seventeen and his mother said,

"Wrap it up, you're not immune." And that was that. He never expected anything more. Mother was her own person, unique in the world. If her brain wasn't so soaked in gin, she might have been a genius. But alcohol meant that Einstein wouldn't turn in his grave.

Dad, contrary to popular belief, was a stickler for tradition. "Shag whatever boy you want," he used to say, "so long as you put a ring on some girl's finger before you're thirty."

He was concerned with his business, which extended to all eight daily newspapers, thirty-five websites, a twenty-six per cent stake in Trafick, the latest social app to hit the scene, and an up-and-coming news station on satellite TV. "No son of mine will waste his life in the butt-crack of another man. You'll make an honest woman of some poor girl, the way I did with your mother."

Honest, my arse, Oliver thought.

He showered, and when Annabelle knocked on his bedroom door to tell him the car was here, he had dressed in a classically cut blue suit that was tailored for him just last week.

"Remind me why I'm doing this?" he asked her as she straightened his tie.

"To get away from your perverse family and friends," she said. Her Christmas hairband had light-up stars on it.

"You can't possibly need a break from your family, too."

"My mum's doing this charity event. She won't even know I'm gone." Oliver knew not to ask about her father. He'd walked out on her when she was a child.

Annabelle said, "One night on a steam train will be like an eternity in heaven."

"Can't they slow the train down? Make it two nights?"

"I'll ask the driver."

"Did you give them my rider?"

Annabelle, his personal assistant, pretended to check off a list of items on the palm of her hand. "Fourteen litres of rocky road, one bowl of M&Ms—only the yellow ones—six bottles of spring water from the Outer Hebrides and the blood of seven virgins."

"Just seven?"

"I thought you were on a diet."

"Make it eight, I need the iron."

Annabelle stepped back and inspected him. "You'll do." She opened his bedroom door and looked out before turning back to him. "I've made Grace take Shiva into the garden to look for Santa's robins, and your mother has sequestered herself in her quarters. Scott has brought the car around and you're good to go without making a scene."

"How could I live without you?"

"I'll expect your gratitude expressed in a wonderfully sincere Christmas card."

"You write all my Christmas cards," Oliver said.

Her smile was wide. "Thank you for the gift basket."

On the ride to Dublin Connolly from their South

Dublin home, Oliver Lloyd made a point of switching off his phone and handing it to Annabelle. He never checked it anyway. His P.A. managed his social media apps and anyone who needed to get in touch with him called her direct. He might as well not have a phone.

Belle—and he was the only one who could call her that—screened his calls and texts, and even told him on the rare occasion when a media contact reached out via a social app. He never looked at his DMs. Not since he was fifteen and some woman sent him pictures of her Brazilian, which was the last thing he wanted to see. He had thrown his phone at his mother and said, "I'm never looking at a direct message again."

Mother made it go away. The forty-year-old woman was tracked down by her IP address and arrested. Oliver never found out what happened to her, but Mother hired a P.A. for him soon after. And now he didn't know how many followers he had, or how many of them were crazy women who wanted to share close-up pictures of their intimate parts.

"Pity the world isn't full of crazy *men* willing to share their private photos, eh?" Annabelle often said as she scrolled through his DMs.

But he was pretty much done with men, too. Walt made sure of that. They had known each other for fourteen months, dating for a while before Walt flew off the handle and left him, then crawled back a week later with a little baggie of coke and a bottle of Château Latour. They'd have make-up sex and drink wine, and by morning Oliver would feel alive again and happy with life and love. And two months later Walter Mason was pictured online with another skinny twink who couldn't spell his own name, let alone know if he was being used or not.

Not that Oliver knew that he was being used. Not at first. Breaking up with the money-hungry asshole and checking himself into rehab was the best thing he ever did. Today, he was 194 days sober. He was awarded his six-month chip last week.

The car pulled up outside the rear entrance of Dublin Connolly Station and Annabelle got out to scout ahead. When she waved from the archway that led into the back of the building, Oliver unbuckled his seatbelt, smacked Scott on the shoulder, and said, "I'll make my own way back tomorrow. Tell mother I'll buy her a home in Milan if she can get through the night without calling Annabelle."

"I will make it my duty to get her drunk before she picks up a phone, sir."

Oliver loved that Irish sense of humour. He'd spent a few years in England with his parents when he was young, and if an employee had spoken out of turn, they'd be sacked on the spot. In Ireland, it was expected. Though some men are rich, no man is above a good ribbing. If your friend is not taking the mickey out of you, is he really your friend?

He was ushered from the car into what the station manager called the Green Room, because that was a media thing. The room was neither green nor roomlike. Broom cupboard was more accurate.

The rest of the evening was a blur. He drank two litres of sparkling water, watched the news about the luxury steam train on RTE 1, muted the TV when they mentioned him and Walter Mason, and then paced up and down for the next hour.

He cut the thick red ribbon for national television with a pair of oversized scissors and spent almost thirty minutes holding the whistle's pullcord and smiling for the cameras. They even had him photographed holding a shovelful of coal for the steam engine, which made him look stupid. No one wears a blue suit to a coal-shovelling event.

When the train purred to life and the TV crews were left outside on the platform, Oliver was shown to his private carriage, a retrofitted sleeper car with seven cabins, two bathrooms, a lounge, private kitchen and bar area with dedicated staff. He asked for a glass of orange juice and the barman looked confused.

"With vodka, sir?"

Oliver shook his head. To Annabelle, he said, "Remind me why I'm doing this?"

"The blood of seven virgins."

"Eight."

"Eight. Got it."

He took his orange juice—poured reluctantly—and sat by the window. "Seven hours and forty minutes," he said. "When we get off this train tomorrow morning, we can start a new life in a new country. Let's not go home."

"'New country' makes it sound foreign."

"It might as well be." Northern Ireland was a whole new world for him. He had travelled the globe, shopped in multiple cities and in many languages, but he'd never entered Northern Ireland, which was strange, considering how close it was. Two hours by a normal train. Almost eight hours for *The Duchess of Dublin*.

The train whistled its intention to stop. Oliver Lloyd looked out of the window. As the train slowed, he read the station name. Clannon Station. They hadn't been travelling more than a quarter of an hour and already they were stopping. No wonder it would take so long to get to Belfast.

As he stared at the busy platform, he couldn't make out a single face in the crowd. He was pleased his carriage was in the middle of the train; he could look out without grabbing attention and he was safe in the knowledge that people on board had enough provisions on either side of him to care who was in the middle carriage.

"Eight virgins," he said, raising his glass to Annabelle.

She clinked with him and sipped from her glass of orange squash—if he was off the booze, so was she, by her own choice.

"Let's make it nine virgins," she said. "It's a special occasion."

"Here's to special occasions," Oliver Lloyd said. And even his private barman smiled.

3.

DENIS

D enis didn't want to move, but his left leg was cramping. Tom hadn't said a word since the train started moving, and Denis enjoyed the shared silence and the closeness of Tom's body. But the shocking jolt of his tightened calf muscle made him yelp and he rolled from his hiding place. Beneath him, the train chugged in time with the beating of his heart.

"You okay?"

On his back, Denis nodded and pulled his knee up to flex his foot and stretch out the cramping muscle and the pulsing pain subsided. He stared at the dark ceiling. There was a row of dim nightlights from one end of the luggage car to the other, but their grey luminescence didn't extend to the ground. He dug his phone from his pocket and flicked the flashlight on.

"Careful where you point that," Tom said, shielding his eyes and blinking. He was attractive even when he scrunched up his face.

They'd been on board for only twenty minutes and the gentle rocking of the train carriage was soothing. "Are we even moving?"

"Must be going pretty slow," Tom agreed.

A couple of times since they boarded, the train had slowed as though it was going to stop, and panic rose in Denis' throat in case an attendant opened the carriage door and discovered them in an illicit tryst, but after a few moments, the train rolled forward again.

Denis dug around in his backpack when his stomach cried out for food. He hadn't finished dinner when his mum asked him about his love life. In his haste to leave her house, he didn't pack anything edible except a flapjack that had been sitting on his bedside locker next to an untouched cup of tea that, by the time he was leaving, had formed a thin layer of skin on the top.

As Tom scuttled out from his hiding place, Denis tore the wrapper open and broke off the end of the flapjack, handing half to Tom.

It was gooey and chalky and hard to swallow. But it was food.

Tom studied the sticky treat and Denis said, "It's not as nice as homemade, but it's something."

Chewing, Tom said, "My sister makes a good flapjack."

"Dude."

"What?"

"I thought you were making an innuendo."

Tom punched his shoulder. "Piss off. That's my sister." He settled down beside Denis and sucked the sticky residue from his fingertips. Denis looked away, with a different sticky taste at the back of his mouth.

To lift his mind out of the sordid gutter, Denis said, "Where's Aaron?"

"Still at Aberystwyth. He's flying home tomorrow."

It'd be good to see him again, Denis thought. They'd been inseparable for years, always giving Aaron's older brother a hard time. Denis even hung out at their house when Aaron was spending the weekend at his dad's and Tom showed him how to play Grand Theft Auto.

When Denis and Aaron would top-and-tail in Aaron's single bed on the few occasions that Denis stayed overnight, he'd lie awake and listen to Tom snoring in the next room. He imagined creeping in and slipping into bed beside him, so quietly that Tom didn't wake, and he'd inhale his masculine scent and fall asleep with an erection that would still be there in the morning.

"We should grab a drink some night before I head back to Dublin."

Tom was never the academic type. He'd escaped school as soon as he could and went straight into Al's Garage. Growing up, he was always tinkering with things. Neighbourhood kids brought him their bikes and he'd adjust the chain cogs for speed.

Denis was convinced Tom was born with a greasy spanner in his hands.

He wrapped what was left of the flapjack and buried it at the bottom of his pack. It didn't taste as sweet as it should, but he wasn't sure if the flapjack had soured or his tastebuds were tired.

The suitcases around them might contain some food, maybe a bottle of wine to rinse the caviar down—given the rich appearance of the passengers, he was certain to find the crown jewels in one of these cases if he hunted hard enough.

Denis ran his fingertip over the nearest piece of luggage, an oversized hard-shell case that you could fit a man in, but he couldn't bring himself to open it. These were people's private belongings, and they were trusting the train staff not to let a couple of stowaways rifle through them.

Denis stood up and steadied himself against a crate as the train shuddered and rocked beneath them. He'd been on a steam train once, one Christmas before Dad died when, as a family, they took a special Santa train. Kids were excited when Santa strode through the carriages, handing out small gifts, but Denis was more concerned with listening to the train as it chugged along to a repetitive beat. He stood in the aisle between the worn seats, holding on to nothing, balancing as the train wobbled and he counted the beats of the rocking motion.

When Santa crouched and asked what he was doing, Denis said, "Being the train." And Santa laughed, because what other response could you give to a six-year-old?

Denis couldn't remember what silly present the skinny man in a fat suit gave him that year. But he remembered his father picking him up and hoisting him onto his shoulders as they left the train and went back to their car. He had felt safe there, so high up but secure as the world passed beneath his father's shoes.

He counted the beats of the rumbling train and stilled his mind. Memories have little point if they make you sad, and Denis' memories were a collection of sadness, a life so beholden to secrets—his, Mum's, the secret Dad took to his grave about why he killed himself—that he wanted to bundle up all his memories and stuff them into the bottom of a bag with a half-eaten flapjack and bury it under a mountain.

As he felt the train ease around a bend in the track, Denis knew they couldn't go all night without something to eat.

"We can't stay here forever, can we?"

Tom struggled to his feet and ducked under an overhanging shelf. When he stood beside Denis, he was at least half a head taller.

"We'll go into the next carriage," Tom said. "But when we open the door, we have to move fast. Straight through, okay? We don't linger by the door unless you want to get caught."

They shuffled towards the end of the carriage, using the flashlight on Denis' phone to guide them, and Tom felt for the door handle or a release mechanism that would let them into the next carriage. Denis worried they were trapped, but Tom's fingers slid over a button on the wall beside the door. It swished open and, in the darkness, Denis had expected to see the night sky above him as, like a cowboy in some ancient Western movie, he jumped from one carriage to the next. But the area between the connecting carriages was encased, with a flexible floor and walls that moved with each bend.

He put his ear to the door of the next carriage but all he could hear was the train's powerful breathing as it climbed a hill. There was nothing else to do; either they opened the door and strode into the carriage as though they belonged there, or they returned to the confines of the luggage area to spend the next eight hours in isolation.

Denis straightened his hoodie, adjusted the backpack on his shoulder, and nodded. Tom pressed the door's release button.

They stepped inside, Denis keeping his head down, and marched with purpose away from the door as he heard it sweep closed behind them. He looked up, and when he did, his eyes widened. It was like he had stepped into the 1800s. The train was wider than he had imagined, and on one side was a row of cabins, plush red curtains hiding whatever lay beyond their dark wooden doors. Along the opposite wall were a series of chairs and couches, dining tables and, further up, a bar with two staff members serving the revellers. A Christmas tree stood tall and proud in the corner.

Plucky music tinkled out of hidden speakers and stirred up memories of old Charlie Chaplin movies that his dad had loved.

"Woah," Tom said.

Among the well-dressed passengers who milled around in groups, Denis felt out of place. He followed Tom towards the bar area, excusing himself when he had to squeeze past a gibbon of laughing men. When a waiter approached, Denis turned to walk the other way, but the man said, "Champagne?"

"Don't mind if I do," Tom said.

Denis faced the waiter and, smiling, took a glass from the tray. Holding it, he felt a little less uncomfortable. The champagne was dry and tart. A waitress held out a tray with a selection of finger foods—little dollops of green paste on thin crackers, something that looked like a cocktail sausage pinned to an olive—and they helped themselves. Denis took one of the crackers. He wasn't sure what the green substance was—wasabi, perhaps—but on an empty stomach, it was more delicious than a stale flapjack. Before she turned away, he took another.

"This is the life," Tom said. He clinked glasses with Denis, then said, "I'm going to follow that waitress. Maybe she'll give me her number."

Denis sat in a bucket chair near one of the windows and watched Tom disappear into the crowd. He looked out, but it was too dark to see much other than the reflection of the 1800s roaring party that they had managed to gate-crash. But at least it was warmer here than the luggage carriage, and the platters of food seemed to be complimentary. He grabbed a minuscule sandwich from a passing tray and two chicken vol-au-vents from another.

When someone sat in the seat to his right, close enough to be uncomfortable, Denis was afraid to look up.

"This is madness," the girl said. "It's like we've stepped back in time."

Denis glanced at her, nodded his agreement, and pushed one of his delicious snacks into his mouth to prove that he couldn't talk right now.

"Did your parents force you to come along, too?" she asked. She looked to be Denis' age or a little older. While Denis chewed, she pressed on. "I think they're desperately trying to have one final family trip together that doesn't end in disaster. And that's just pathetic because as soon as we get home, they're getting a divorce. They think I don't know, but I do. That's them, over there. You can tell they can't stand each other, can't you? Which are yours?"

With a noncommittal flourish of his hand, Denis indicated the largest gathering of adults in the carriage.

"At least they didn't make you dress up. I haven't worn a dress since my Confirmation. What are you eating? It looks disgusting."

"It's nice," Denis said.

"Oh, it speaks."

"When it needs to."

"Which room are you in? Did they put you in with your parents or have you got a bunk of your own?"

Denis didn't get a chance to answer, but he wasn't sure which was worse—his inability to tell her which room he was supposed to be staying in, or the ticket inspector who had just entered their carriage.

"Tickets, please," the old man shouted above the din of pleasure, and the train rocked as though to shake Denis free of his chair.

He stood up. "I'm going to go find some more of these little chicken things."

"Vol-au-vents," the girl told him. "Come find me after your parents pass out from too much booze. Cabin Three."

He gave her the smallest wave as he turned away. He had no idea how he was going to get out of this situation, or where Tom had disappeared to. Maybe he should have asked the girl to hide him in her room.

The old man in his bottle-green uniform was getting closer, inspecting the tickets of the partygoers, and calling for their attention every few steps. "Tickets. Tickets, please."

Denis slipped his backpack off his shoulder and pretended to root around inside it, but he knew that ruse wouldn't work. He looked up and saw that the old man was talking to the nearest group of adults.

Denis tried one of the doors that contained the passengers' sleeping quarters, but it was locked, the brass handle unyielding.

He inched towards the partiers that he'd said his parents belonged to, and when the old ticket inspector approached, Denis crouched to tie his shoelace.

His heart was racing and, down on one knee, he felt the blast of warm air from a heating vent as it washed his face in the heat of shame.

"Tickets, please."

Denis pushed forward out of his sprinter's starting position, backpack gripped in one hand and tried to look casual as he eased through the crowd behind the inspector. He had done it.

"There you are," Tom said. "Come on, we need to move further up the train." He waved a piece of paper in front of Denis' face and grinned.

"Instead of shagging the staff, maybe ask her for a couple of free tickets."

"Don't be jealous, Denny. Besides, I saw you talking to that girl. Let's get out of the ticket inspector's way first, then you can go back for her later."

Denis nudged his way to the carriage door, slapping the release button several times before the door slid open, and they stepped through the gap between carriages and into the subsequent car with as much fortified grace as they could muster.

The door closed behind them, and Denis breathed.

This second carriage was nothing like the previous one. As he looked around, it was futuristic in décor. The walls were polished chrome, and the floor had an ornate marble effect. The waiters were dressed the same, but even the passengers appeared less formal than in the first carriage, and they were more jovial. Perhaps the alcohol in this car was stronger. Strands of twinkling lights were wrapped around the chrome uprights and a Christmas tree near the closest window was dropping pine needles on the floor.

On the walls between the cabins, large TVs replayed the train's departure from Dublin, with an attractive young man in a blue suit cutting the ribbon, using a pair of giant scissors. Denis thought he recognised him but couldn't be sure. The moving ticker along the bottom of the screen read: *Premier luxury overnight rail service a first for Ireland. Cross-border prosperity open to all.*

Beyond him, on the ceiling, swaying with the motion of the train, a giant chandelier looked as though it could fall and crush the people standing under it at any minute.

Tom sought out the waitresses with their trays of food and slapped Denis on the back. "I reckon I'll sample the food in every single carriage."

"I don't think it's the food you want to be sampling."

Tom winked.

A sign above the bar read, *Tickets must be presented when placing food or drink orders.* But as long as the waitresses circled with their platters of goodies, Denis was content to stand beside Tom and watch the night roll by. Tom's presence gave him a sense of security.

And they were far enough out of Clannon village that Denis could finally breathe.

4.

OLIVER

Why am I here? The thought turned over in Oliver's head in time with the train's puffing hydraulics. And then the answer: better here than anywhere else.

The realisation that he was cut off from everyone who made him feel less than perfect hit him with excitement and, taking a moment to settle his stomach, he smiled. Mum, Dad, Grace, Walter. He was free from them all for the next eight hours. That was the best Christmas present he has ever given himself.

"Why are you looking so smug?" Annabelle asked. She sat at the edge of the long bar, skimming through his social media apps on her iPad, a steaming cup of black coffee beside her as she replied to users' comments and cleaned out his direct message folders.

"I'm free."

"Congratulations." Her fingers whipped across the screen. "Channel Four have emailed again."

"The answer is still no. How many times a year do you want me to be on TV, Belle?"

"As many times as you want, Ollie, but the money is good and the power you'd get from your appearance would help your standing."

"My standing is fine. It's my lying down that needs work."

"You and me both, sweetie," Annabelle said with that sex-starved exasperation he was used to hearing in her voice. Working as his P.A. for the last two years gave her little time for her own relationships, and he wished she'd take a step back. He was a job to her—and a friend—but a job, nonetheless. Annabelle needed to switch off as much as Oliver did sometimes.

"Besides," Oliver said, "I don't need the money, and who wants power?"

"I'd be happy with either. You're an anomaly, Ollie. You're number four in the Top 30 Under 30, you're so rich you don't even know how much you're worth, and I swear you'd give it all away for a cookie."

"I have a sweet tooth."

The joke was insincere, but Annabelle was right. Oliver Lloyd did not like the attention that his father's fortune had thrust on him. The world's tabloid media picked through his trash, women wanted to go down on him, and the only men he could attract were greedy junkies like Walter Mason. He would give it all up, every single cent, for a quiet life away from public scrutiny. He wondered what it would be like to sneeze without the press analysing his facial expressions in detail.

He stepped from the bar to one of the larger windows. In this executive carriage, the glass was tinted, and with the darkness of a late December evening, he could just about make out the crescent moon as it squatted between the silver clouds. The horizon, a steady constant, was a blur of shadows.

He was bored. He checked his watch—a simple Swatch with an army-green strap—and was disappointed to learn they hadn't even been on board for an hour yet. They had arranged a walkthrough of the train for him at midnight, a casual meet-and-greet that he was not looking forward to. He'd spend an hour with a smile hurting his cheeks, letting people take selfies with him, invading his personal space and spreading his image all over social media. It wasn't people he disliked—some of them, like Annabelle, were nice; it was the sense of celebrity that he abhorred. He wanted to make a difference in the world for something he did, not something he was.

His reflection in the window shone like a ghost haunting the train. "You get me," Oliver told it. "You're the only one who does."

"Every time you talk to yourself, a fairy dies," Annabelle said. She didn't look up.

Growing up with a desire to hide from the world's attention, Oliver talked to himself a lot. "When you're too busy to talk to me, what do you want me to do?" He didn't have many friends outside of school. When people found out who he was, they were either intimidated by him or sought him out only for the pleasures of his money.

Oliver paced the carriage and back. "I need a disguise."

"You need to sit down; you're making me nervous."

To the barman, Oliver asked, "Adam, are there any shops onboard?"

"There's a souvenir shop in Carriage C, sir, but all they sell is keyrings, knitted scarves and model trains."

"Why do you need a disguise?" Annabelle asked. She sat her iPad down and looked at him with little patience on her face.

"I'm bored. I want to explore the train without being recognised."

"Sweetheart, you could wear a chadaree and you'd still be recognisable." She pushed his phone across the bar to him. "Here, play a game or call your mother."

"Just find me something to wear, Belle. The more you stall, the more bored I get. And don't threaten me with my mother or I'll kick you off a moving train."

"I'd like to see you try," she laughed. But she stood up and went to the connecting door. "It's a mistake, believe me, but I'll be back with some clown shoes and a tutu in no time."

The barman, Adam, poured him another orange juice

and Oliver could tell he wanted to say something. He sat, resigned.

"I think it was a good thing you did, saving that whale. Anyone else in your position would have just thrown money at it and said they did their bit. But you got straight in there to help."

Oliver nodded. He had anticipated a request for an autograph or a selfie, not a commendation. The Sperm whale, nicknamed Spunky by the local media, had swum up the River Liffey and made it as far as Temple Bar a couple of years ago. Oliver had been drinking that Sunday afternoon nearby when he heard the commotion on the riverfront. When he went to investigate, two coastguard rafts were trying to turn the whale around. Oliver called Annabelle who had a speedboat out to him in ten minutes. When the whale beached in shallow water, Oliver was one of the first to help keep it wet with hoses and buckets of water.

By two A.M. Monday morning, when the whale was freed and swimming towards the ocean, Oliver's suede shoes were ruined and the legs of his jeans were soaked, but he was happy he had helped rescue the poor creature.

Of course, the media ate it up and for two weeks he was pictured in all the glossy magazines. *Oliver Lloyd Gets Spunky. Lloyd Releases Sperm.* And *The Party-Boy and the Sperm Whale: The Inside Scoop.*

They took a good deed and turned it into a joke.

But the barman remembered it as an act of kindness, and Oliver was grateful. "Thank you," he said. "I just did what I could."

He took his drink across the carriage to inspect the cabins. They were spacious for such a small area, with a queen bed in each, a minibar, desk and hidden shower stall. It was no five-star hotel, but the fact they could pack all this onto a train surprised him.

In each of the seven cabins, a wall-mounted monitor revealed a dinner and drinks menu, as well as a map in the corner of the screen with a live GPS update of the train's location. They hadn't even hit Drogheda yet.

On the nightstand beside each bed was a complimentary eye mask and bottle of artesian spring water, as well as a manicure set and sewing kit. The obligatory foil-wrapped chocolates rested on the pillows and, behind the door, two towelling robes with *The Duchess of Dublin* embroidered on the breast. If it wasn't for the incessant rocking of the train and the noise of her powerful chuffing, Oliver would be forgiven for thinking he wasn't in a moving carriage.

He tested the bed. It was comfortable yet firm.

When Annabelle came back into the carriage, he met her at the bar and raised an eyebrow. "Did you steal that from an old woman?"

The coat she held out for him was bright green and padded, and she carried a flat-brimmed black fedora with leather trim.

"I couldn't find any clown makeup," she said.

"Where did you get these—a joke shop?"

"I paid a man for them. Hey, you're the one that

wants to go exploring."

"So, my choices are walking through the train as Oliver Lloyd and getting mobbed, or Oliver Hardy's long-lost sister who got dressed in the dark after her eyes were poked out by an angry bear?"

"I don't envy your choice, but it's yours to make."

Oliver put the coat on and buttoned it. When he pulled the hat over his head and looked at his ghostly reflection in the window, he laughed. "What do I look like?"

"Like an angel," Annabelle said.

From behind the bar, Adam said, "Oliver Hardy's ugly sister is more attractive than she thinks, sir."

"I said she was long-lost, not ugly."

"My mistake," he smirked.

Oliver turned from his reflection and marched to the door. "Are you coming?"

"Hold on," Annabelle said. "I'm just getting the camera ready. Instagram is going to love this."

"Haven't I already threatened to kick you off the train today?"

"Only once," she said.

Oliver pushed the button to open the door.

5.

DENIS

They had stepped from the 1800s into the future. As Tom walked among the crowd, Denis couldn't take his eyes off the huge chandelier that swung from the ceiling.

"Impressive, isn't she?" the waiter nearest him said. "Six hundred and seventy pieces of real crystal and a series of polished tungsten tubes. Guess her weight. Go on, have a guess."

Denis shrugged.

"Five hundred pounds. Suspended above your head."

"What happens if it falls?"

The waiter held out his tray of minuscule hamburgers, each one pinned together with a toothpick topped by a tiny paper flag with the train's logo on it. "Better eat up before we find out."

Denis took two. He skirted the chandelier with a series of hurried steps, and when he looked around for Tom, he found him laughing with one of the young passengers as though he had no concern for being caught without a ticket. When a waitress came close with a tray of drinks, Denis smiled at her; the universal non-verbal indicator for *I'll have one of those, please.*

Mini-burger and champagne flute in hand, he felt safe knowing that the ticket inspector was behind him. His hood was down, and he was relaxed enough to feel a level of satisfaction that he was unfamiliar with. He was one person among a hundred in the carriage, any one of which could be his mother if he was questioned by someone in authority. "There she is, over there," he'd say, and then disappear when the inspector turned to look.

But thinking about his mother soured his mood. He drank the entire glass of champagne and beckoned for another. When he settled on an angular sofa by the west-facing windows, he stared out at the night and could only see his own sad face looking back. "Shut up," he said.

He hadn't noticed any relationship issues between his parents when he was growing up. They weren't rich, but they never seemed to struggle for money, and when he tore holes in the knees of his school trousers, he never had to go to class in a pair of black jeans like some kids. Dad was happy most of the time, especially in the days preceding his suicide. It was a lifetime ago, but Denis could recall every detail of those weeks. Dad took some time off work and they clambered into the car for a caravan holiday up north at The Downings.

Dad woke him with a gentle nudge of the shoulder that first morning when it was still dark, and he put his finger to his lips for quiet. "Don't wake the girls," he'd said. "We're going fishing."

"What time's it?"

"Time to catch the worm," Dad said.

While he didn't appreciate being woken before five A.M., Denis had to admit the sunrise at their backs made the bay shimmer like glitter. They stayed there, wearing waders, standing in the water where some old man had told them was the best place for a catch, and they fished for five hours. Not that they caught anything. When they were done, Denis' toes were wrinkled from the prolonged water exposure, and Dad wrapped him in a thick towel that felt like the warmest hug in the world.

On the way back to the caravan, Dad gave Denis a piggyback and said they'd stop at the market and buy a couple of salmon so Mum and Caroline would never know the truth.

"Can we name them?" Denis remembered asking.

Dad said, "They've already got names. They're called Mum and Caroline."

Denis laughed, and Dad laughed, and the man at the market laughed when Denis told him their plan.

A week before his father's suicide, it seemed like the whole world was laughing. And then nobody knew how to laugh anymore. Caravans and fishing and piggy-backs were gone. In their place were Mum's sad eyes and Caroline's tears. Boys in his class no longer asked him to play football and teachers forgot to care if he didn't do his homework.

And outside the train, the reflection of a sad boy stared back at him.

When Tom came back with a plateful of chips, Denis said, "How did you get hold of those?" He took a hand-ful when Tom offered.

"You just have to look like you belong. Head up, big smile. People don't second-guess you if you're not sec-ond-guessing yourself."

"Excuse me," an elderly lady said. She eyed the greasy smear on Tom's cheek and the grubbiness of his hands. "Do you work here? The lightbulb in my cabin has blown and I can't see a damn thing."

Tom wiped his lips with the side of his hand and thrust the plate of chips towards Denis.

"Of course, madam. Which cabin is yours?"

She pointed.

"I'll be right over with a replacement bulb, madam. Please, help yourself to the complimentary snacks."

"What a nice young man," the old woman said as she walked away.

Tom winked at Denis.

"She thinks you're an engineer?" Denis asked.

Tom inspected his hands. His fingernails were black and oil stains were smeared across his skin. "Good job I didn't wash my hands, eh? I'll be back in a minute."

"You're not really going to fix her lightbulb, are you?"

"Why not? You heard her—she can't see a damn thing. Besides, I like an older woman."

"You like all women."

"I promise to leave one or two for you," Tom said as he slipped between the crowd of passengers.

Denis returned his gaze to the window. It was clear Tom was never going to have any interest in him, and the loneliness of his life caved in around him again. Maybe it was the sadness flooding his face or the fact that he wasn't engaged in raucous laughter with a maddening group of other grownups, or perhaps he looked like a responsible adult, but when he looked away from his reflection, he saw a young boy standing beside him, wide eyes brimmed with tears and redness, his fingertip between his lips.

"I can't find my nammy," he said.

"Your mammy?"

"I can't find my mammy or my nammy."

Denis looked around. Nobody cared about the abandoned child. Or the little boy beside him.

"What's your name?"

"Do you know where my nammy is?"

"Maybe we can find your nammy. Or your mammy," Denis said. He stood up, slid his glass onto a table, and reached his hand out for the child to take it. "I'm Denis. Is your mum over there?"

The kid looked where Denis pointed, then shrugged.

Denis was torn—scour the train for the boy's mother and risk being caught without a ticket or pass the lad off on the nearest waitress. But when the little boy gripped his outstretched hand, the deal was sealed.

"Sorry to interrupt. I'm trying to find this boy's mum."

The group of adults he spoke to glanced at them, shook their heads the way you do when a charity volunteer asks if you have two minutes to spare, and returned to their conversation.

Denis stopped himself from telling the kid that he was better off without his nammy. He'd learn, one day.

He hunkered down and smiled. "Can you tell me what your nammy looks like?"

The boy looked around at the grownups. "She's bigger than her," he said, pointing.

Denis was quick to lower the boy's accusatory finger unless they both got thrown off the train. "Do you want to tell me your name now?"

The lad leaned in and cupped Denis' ear. He whispered, "Jamie Collins."

"Okay, Jamie Collins. Let's walk up the train and if you spot your mammy or your nammy, you tell me, okay?"

Jamie nodded. He took Denis' hand again and they squeezed through the throng of passengers. As they walked the carriage, Denis reassured him that they'd find his parents. And he was convinced they would; it's not like they threw their kid onto a passing train and ran. They were here somewhere.

"Excuse me, do you recognise this little boy? He's lost."

No one knew him. They walked on.

When they came to the bar, Denis lifted the boy by the armpits and held him up for the barman's inspection. "Do you know if anyone's lost a kid?"

The barman shrugged, disinterested. "Maybe try one of the ticket inspectors."

At the door to the next carriage, Denis turned and said, "Are you sure they're not in this car?"

Jamie's wide eyes scanned the room. When his chin trembled, Denis crouched and rubbed the kid's back. "It's okay. We'll find them. It's a big train. Did you come through this door?"

Jamie shrugged.

"How many doors did you come through?"

He shrugged again.

Denis pushed the release button. As he turned to enter the next carriage, Tom was coming towards him with a box of lightbulbs in his hand.

"No shit, man, where did you get those?"

Tom said, "Don't ask, don't tell. Who's the kid?"

"He got lost. We're looking for his mum."

Tom cupped his hand and made an obscene gesture. "Maybe she'll give you a handy-J for returning him."

Denis and his tearful charge entered the next carriage. As the door swished closed behind them, Denis whistled. The first carriage had an 1800s theme and the second was futuristic. This third one had Halloween décor, which explained the three witches he saw at Clannon Station. The walls were painted black and there were glow-in-the-dark skeletons hanging from the ceiling, which made the solitary Christmas tree seem out of place. The passengers were in costume and the theme tune from *The Munsters* was playing on the speakers.

Jamie Collins clung to Denis' leg.

"It's okay, kid. I hate Halloween, too." He picked Jamie up into his arms. Given that the boy was not in fancy dress, he was pretty sure he hadn't come from this carriage. But if his parents weren't in the previous car either, Jamie could have come from any of the subsequent cars.

"Your nammy must be going out of her mind."

Jamie nodded and smiled. At least he wasn't crying anymore.

They rushed through the Halloween car and Denis let Jamie push the door-release button. He smacked it until it opened. In the new carriage, they relaxed. Denis felt the boy's muscles ease as Jamie clung to his neck. They were in what appeared to be an underwater-themed car. The blue walls shimmered from invisible lighting strips, and there was a fishing net pinned across the ceiling. The waitresses were dressed as mermaids, with clamshell bikini bras and Santa hats, their feet poking out of their fish-scale tails, and the passengers were wearing normal clothes, nothing fancy. Nothing fishy.

"Nammy," Jamie shouted, and his arms left Denis' neck and reached out for someone further up the carriage.

"Do you see your parents?" He let Jamie squirm to the ground but kept a close hold of his hand. Jamie led him through the throng of underwater partygoers.

"Jamie, where the heck have you been?" a large woman said. She glanced at Denis before scooping Jamie into her arms.

"He was two cars back. I'm sorry; he kept asking for his nammy?"

"I'm his nammy," the woman said. "And this here is his mammy."

Denis had no response. The little kid had two mothers. As if one wasn't enough. It didn't strike him immediately that they were a lesbian couple, but when he made the realisation, the woman narrowed her eyes, and he could almost sense her mood shift. How many times had she defended her family from the questioning gaze of strangers?

To break the gloom that settled over them, Denis poked Jamie in the ribs. "You happy now?"

"Thank you," Jamie said, and he put his arms around Denis' neck for a hug.

"Where are our manners?" Jamie's nammy said as his mammy took their child from her. "Thank you, so much. We honestly didn't even notice he had wandered off. How far can you get on a train?"

"That's okay. I'm glad we found you." He nodded at them, backing away, but the large woman beckoned him close.

"If it wasn't for you, he could have jumped off the back of the train or—Mother, say thank you."

"Thank you," Jamie's mammy said.

"What's going on?" a passing stranger asked.

Denis' face flushed red. This was too much attention. He pointed behind him as if he needed to get back to his own car, but Jamie's nammy gripped the sleeve of his hoodie.

"We owe you a drink. Or money. We should give you some money. Where's my bag?"

"You don't need to, honestly."

"Nonsense. I wish your parents were here so we could thank them for raising such a responsible young man."

"Seriously, I'm just glad Jamie's back with his parents." He didn't know what else to say to end this show of gratitude and release him. Other passengers were pooling around them, and Denis now knew what it felt like to be a celebrity.

"What happened?" someone asked.

"Our son wandered off and this lad brought him back to us."

"Fantastic news," a woman said.

"Humanity is not lost," someone announced.

One of the train's inspectors fought through the gathered crowd. "What's going on here?" he asked.

Jamie's nammy said, "This young man saved our son."

"I just walked him through the train until we found his parents," Denis said. Having a train official standing so close made his cheeks flush. He wished Tom was there to help him out.

A waiter with a tray of vol-au-vents said, "Praise be."

"I don't think I've seen you yet, son. I'd better just check your ticket."

"We should give him some money," Jamie's nammy said.

"If you give me your ticket, I'll arrange a free drink for you," the inspector said.

"It's fine, honestly. I'm just glad he's back with his parents."

"You did a good deed, son. Just hand me your ticket."

"No, honestly," Denis pleaded. He wondered, for a second, how thick the glass windows were. Could he jump through one the way they did in the movies? Land on his back and roll to a stop before leaping to his feet and sprinting into the forest?

"Just give me your ticket, son," the inspector said.

Denis rifled through his hoodie pockets. He had forgotten about the twenty Euros his mum had given him. "I think I must've left it in the other carriage with my parents. I'll go and get it."

The waiter said, "Does he not have a ticket?"

Denis looked at him. His life was over. And all he could think to do was steal a fistful of vol-au-vents from the waiter's tray and run. He sprinted up the train carriage, weaving through the crowd. Leaping over a chair, he stumbled, bashed his shin on the corner of a low table, and spun, arms outstretched, turning, falling—he could see the ground coming up towards him, but he couldn't stop it. And he put his hands out, realising at the last second that one of those hands had three warm pastries crushed between his fingers.

And the pale blue carpet struck his forehead.

"Up you come," the ticket inspector said, his fingers gripping the back of Denis' hoodie.

Denis closed his eyes. The game was over.

6.

OLIVER

In his green coat and black fedora, Oliver stepped into the next carriage. He pulled the brim of his hat down over his eyes and waited, but no one screamed his name. The glossy magazines would have a field day if they saw him dressed like this, but he was feeling alone in a big empty carriage and, though he didn't want any human interaction, he wanted to know there were people nearby. The buzz of conversations held a lulling quality that soothed him.

Annabelle whispered, "You'll definitely find someone to shag dressed like that."

"I'm counting on it."

"Now what? Are we just going to stand here?"

Oliver gave it some thought. Now that he was out

of his lonely train car, he wasn't sure why he wanted to stretch his legs in the first place. But he needed to feel part of something bigger than himself and listening to the noise of excitement was enough.

"And it was built in 1903," a man told those people who hung on his every word. Perhaps he was a plant by the train company, a tour guide. "The engine was built in Dublin; did you know that? Designed by Mr McCarthy who was originally from Utah in the United States. Imagine that—an American emigrating to Ireland, not the other way about."

The people around him laughed as though it was a hilarious turn of events.

"Bar?" Annabelle asked.

"Bar."

As they pushed through the milling crowd to get to the bar, he overheard snippets of conversation that hinted at the excitement sweeping through the carriage. Most of the enjoyment was directed at the lavish train— "Can't believe I'm going to be sleeping in a bed. On a train," one kid said—but some of the anticipation was at Oliver's midnight walkthrough.

"Is he really six-foot-four?" a girl asked her mother.

"Don't believe everything you read, Sarah, he's probably shorter than you."

Closer to the bar, a teenage boy told his friend, "Lloyd's just a money-grabbing shit like all the other rich-dick wankers."

"What's a rich dick?" Oliver asked Annabelle.

"The only useful part of a rich man."

"Remind me to give you a pay rise when we get home."

Although he'd had a P.A. since he was fifteen, Annabelle had held the role for only two years. But she was closer in age to him than her predecessor and she got his sensibilities. If she ever got a job somewhere else, he'd be devastated. He imagined that quitting your job was like having a divorce where only one person wanted out of the relationship. You may marry again, eventually, but you'd always compare the new one to the old.

"One orange juice with ice, one lime and soda, please," Annabelle told the barman. She flashed her ticket as discreetly as she could—theirs were the only black tickets onboard, imprinted with gold foil. The train company had told Oliver that, in time, they'd offer black-label tickets to anyone who wished to host a private party in the carriage they'd offered to him, but on its maiden journey, they wanted to keep it lowkey.

Annabelle jammed the ticket back inside the flip-case of her iPad.

When a couple of girls nudged into the bar beside him, Oliver shuffled aside. The girls, nineteen or twenty years old, he guessed, were dressed in skimpy outfits that didn't match the cold season, and their faces were already reddened with alcohol.

"Two gin and tonics," one of the girls shouted at the barman while he was pouring Annabelle's drinks. She turned to Oliver, her phone in hand, and said, "Phone's dead. Have you got the right time? Oliver Lloyd's coming out at midnight."

He checked his watch. "It's almost ten o'clock."

"Fuck's sake, it's ages yet," the girl told her friend. Then she called to the barman again.

To Annabelle, Oliver said, "This Oliver Lloyd bloke better be fit."

"I hear he's hideous. Potbelly, balding head, missing teeth."

Oliver wiggled his eyebrows. "Wrap him up; I'll take two of him."

"I hear his assistant is mighty fine, though."

"They do say he only employs fit people."

"Ain't that the truth." She took her drink from the bar and slid his orange juice towards him.

Oliver wanted to scratch the top of his head where the hat made him itch, but he knew if he took it off, he'd be discovered. The airhead who asked him for the time was still nearby and oblivious.

He was glad they could joke together. Often, Annabelle was the only person in his circle who understood him. She knew his shirt size, how many paparazzi had it in for him, and what was rattling around inside his head most of the time, those thoughts he could never say out loud.

She was the only person in the world who knew that when he was seventeen, he filed for emancipation. He never went through with it, but he got close. It was a desperate time for him when his father was abroad for half the year and his mother was drinking gin in bed all day. His sister was dating three men at the time and his P.A., a man called James, used to show up to meetings with white powder caked at the edges of his nostrils and a mean streak in his voice. It was James that introduced Oliver to the pleasures of cocaine.

Annabelle, his fourth assistant, had become his confidante with such swiftness that it felt as though they'd been friends since birth.

"What comes after 'third time's the charm'?" he'd asked her once.

"Fourth time's the best damn bitch you've ever met."

And she was right. He was grateful to have her at his side.

He sipped his drink as she pulled up his calendar on her tablet.

"When we get back tomorrow, you have a fitting for Shiva's birthday party at four P.M. I haven't bought anything for her because I know you want to keep her separate from everything else."

Shiva, his niece, was the most special person he knew. She superseded even Annabelle and, though his P.A. would order gifts and flowers for anyone else—his mother included—Oliver made a point of taking care of his responsibilities as an uncle.

Like any four-year-old, Shiva was going through a dinosaur-loving phase. She could name over eighty species, and her favourite was the stegosaurus because it had, she informed him, "big teeth along its back." For her upcoming birthday, Oliver had bought her a life-size model, made from fibreglass, which would stand in the garden on the morning of her birthday with a pink bow around its neck.

"I don't see why I need a fitting for a child's birthday party," Oliver said. "Shiva wouldn't care if I rocked up in a sequin dress, so long as I was there."

"I don't need to tell you what Grace would say if you turned up in a dress. Besides, you need a suit that fits the birthday colour scheme."

"Will Prasad be home in time for the party?" No one ever called Shiva's dad by his first name.

"No idea. I'm your P.A., not his."

Oliver turned away and looked across the carriage. Only when he glanced at the windows did he remember he was on a train. The perpetual chugging of the wheels and the occasional whistle had blended into the background with the sounds of a hundred other conversations. This was the lulling atmosphere he had missed while cooped up in his own train car.

"What's after that?" he asked.

Annabelle consulted her iPad. "Mass with your mother on Sunday to commemorate the passing of her father. Then you have a meeting with Abercrombie on Monday morning and your follow-up with Lucia at Alexander McQueen in the afternoon. Tuesday is golf with the Trafick CEO, and Wednesday you're booked in with InStyle Magazine for a photoshoot, then an interview with IQ before you have lunch with Tom Taricci and an afternoon with Lids for Kids."

Lids for Kids IE, a children's cancer charity that made custom hats for the under sixteens in Dublin who were going through chemo, was the only appointment from Annabelle's list that he wanted to keep.

Being a child of the media was not as luxurious as others would have you believe. He seldom had a day to himself.

"Why can't you make a hole and bury me in it? Just dig me up when there's a charity event that's important and tell the others to bugger off."

Annabelle activated Siri on her iPad and said, "Remind me to buy a shovel on Monday."

He was serious. His life wasn't his own. He was a product of the multimedia age, and he couldn't breathe without someone reporting on his every move. Part of him wished he had followed through on his emancipation. If he had, he could be living in a no-name town in a no-name country, miles from anywhere and free from the media. Oliver Lloyd would not be a name on anybody's lips.

"I'm going to kiss him when he walks through here," one of the nearby girls said and interrupted his thoughts.

"He's gay. What makes you think he's going to want you pressed up against his body?" her friend said.

"Roll on the midnight walkthrough," Annabelle whispered to him. She turned to order two more drinks.

As Oliver scanned the carriage, he spotted the usual collection of wealthy families and university students on an expensive bender. A collection of women further down the train car were almost certainly a posh hen party.

When the door opened from the previous carriage and a young man in a hoodie was pushed through in front of a train inspector, Oliver paid attention only because it wasn't something you'd expect to see on a luxury train.

They were too far away for him to understand what was being said, but as the inspector marched the boy up the train, Oliver heard, "I can explain. I have a ticket if you just let me explain."

There was something about the boy's face, something pale and pink and sad, that made Oliver take a step forward.

The inspector said, "Explain it to the conductor as he turfs you off the train."

"Please. You don't understand."

"Save your breath. I've heard it all before. Think you can sneak onto my train without a ticket?"

For a second, the guy's eyes locked with Oliver's and something in the pit of his stomach turned upside down.

Oliver gripped the young man's arm. "There you are. Where the hell have you been?"

The inspector stopped and looked at the stranger in a lime green coat and fedora. "Do you know this delinquent?"

"Take your hands off him," Oliver said. "He's my P.A.'s assistant."

"And you are?"

With momentary reluctance, Oliver removed his hat. "I'm the reason this train ever left Connolly Station."

"Mr Lloyd? My apologies, but he doesn't have a ticket. And if he's your assistant's assistant, why didn't he say so?"

"I tried to say so," the young hoodie-wearing man said, "but you wouldn't let me speak."

"Oh my God," someone screamed. "It's Oliver Lloyd. Oliver Lloyd is in our carriage."

From the corner of his eye, Oliver saw the girl who asked him for the time. Despite the layers of makeup, her face had flushed.

"Where the hell have you been?" Oliver asked the lad.

The guy held up his hand to show one crushed vol-au-vent in the centre of his palm. "I would have brought a whole platter of them if this guy hadn't manhandled me." He shrugged free of the inspector's grip.

Behind the sadness in the stranger's eyes, Oliver saw something more. An interesting expression that he couldn't place. "Can you take your hands off him, please?"

The inspector obliged and Annabelle, ever the peacekeeper, stepped between the hooded man and the official. "I'm so sorry for the mix-up, sir. He's my cousin. I swear; don't ever employ family, right? They're nothing but trouble."

The inspector pouted, his wrinkled lips curling into a scowl. "See that it doesn't happen again."

Oliver said, "I'll keep him under lock and key. You have my word."

Annabelle said, "Trust me, he's not going to be my assistant for long."

The boy, with the vol-au-vent still in his hand, said, "Any chance of a couple more of these?"

And the ticket inspector stomped away.

Oliver looked at the young man, at those deep eyes that spoke a thousand words, and the guy glanced at Annabelle, who was staring at Oliver.

"Can I have your autograph?" someone asked.

"Maybe we should get out of here," Annabelle said.

The guy in the hoodie flipped his backpack over his shoulder and said, "Thanks for the save. See you."

Oliver gripped his arm. "Not a chance. You're coming with us."

7.

DENIS

"I don't even know who you are," Denis said. The tall man in the most ridiculous green puffer coat kept a grip on his sleeve and Denis tried to pull free. He heard the distinct shutter sound of a mobile phone camera, and when he turned to scowl at whoever had taken his photo, he realised the phone—all the phones in the carriage—were not pointed at him but at the man attached to his arm.

He looked at the guy's face, the manicured stubble that framed his jawline and the not-too-prominent cheekbones. They guided Denis' gaze towards his blue eyes that were dark, vibrant and filled with secrets he needed to understand.

He was talking, but Denis couldn't tell what he said.

When he stared at his lips, he recognised a darkness in the pit of his groin that wanted to escape, a feeling that not even Tom had given him.

The girl who said Denis was her cousin, tapped him on the temple. "Are you listening? Let's get a move on."

"Wait. Who are you people?"

The girl got behind him and pushed him towards the connecting door to the next carriage. The tall man strode ahead of them.

"Can we have a selfie, please?"

"I'll be right back, thanks, girls. Just got a situation here."

Denis moved when the young woman pushed him and allowed himself to be carried by her momentum. When the door swished open and she drove him through it into a carriage that was lit with cheerful exuberance, he noticed it was empty even as the door behind them closed.

The tall man pulled his green coat off and threw it into a nearby chair where the shiny fabric made it wilt to the floor like the girls in the previous train car.

"So, you own this train, do you?" Denis asked.

The woman said, "He owns your ass right now, that's for damn sure."

"You can pull the train over and let me off at the next stop."

"Sit down," the man said, and when he spoke, Denis obeyed. "Who the hell do you think you are? You don't even say thanks?"

"You didn't have to do that out there. I was handling it."

"Do you hear that, Annabelle? He was handling it."

"Annabelle knows the score," Denis said, taking a mental note of her name. "I had that ticket inspector just where I wanted him."

Annabelle leaned in, with her hands on the arms of the chair at either side of him, her face inches from his. "Annabelle is not somebody you want to piss off, kid."

"I'm not a kid." He knew his voice was petulant and childlike even as he said it.

"You clearly don't know who you're talking to."

"Leave it, Belle."

"No, Oliver. You just saved his life out there."

"Saved my life?" Denis said. "How dramatic."

"Can I punch him?"

The attractive man she called Oliver pulled her away from Denis' chair. "There'll be no punching anyone. Look, man—what's your name?"

He didn't want to speak but his lips parted regardless. "Denis."

Oliver smiled. It was perfunctory, but it held a warmth that made Denis smile in return. "I'm Oliver. You clearly don't know who I am, and why should you? I'm glad you don't. And maybe I didn't save your life, but that inspector was going to boot you off the train, and then where would you be?" He pointed at the dark windows. "Out there, in the middle of God knows where, three days before Christmas with nothing but a hoodie and a crushed vol-au-vent."

Denis inspected his hand. He'd forgotten about the mess of food between his fingers. When he looked up, Oliver was holding out his pocket square. He took it, wiped his fingers, and handed it back.

"Keep it."

He stuffed it in the front pocket of his hoodie and couldn't hold Oliver's gaze. He never could, with any man he was attracted to. He looked at Annabelle, at the withered coat on the floor, at the barman who was studying their exchange with fascination.

If Oliver wasn't the train's owner, why did he have a private carriage with his own staff? He knew he recognised his face, but couldn't think where he'd seen him, apart from the footage of him cutting the ribbon before the train left Dublin.

Oliver said something.

"I still think we should throw him off," Annabelle said.

Denis kept his head down and his hands in his pockets. He rubbed the silky fabric of Oliver's handkerchief and wondered what it smelled like.

"Step away, Belle. Why don't you get him a glass of water?"

"Got anything stronger?" Denis asked without looking up.

Annabelle stomped to the bar and came back with a bottle of beer. She handed it to Oliver who held it out with one finger and thumb as though the green bottle offended him.

Denis took it, nursed it, but did not drink. On that caravan holiday with his parents, when they were on their way home from their fishing trip, Dad carried two fresh salmon. He presented them to Denis' mother without a word.

"You caught these?" She gutted them and fried them on the small stove and Dad went to the local burger van for a large bag of chips. The four of them gathered around the tiny dining table in their caravan and ate fresh fish with fat chips, and when Mum wasn't looking, Dad handed Denis his bottle of beer. He put his finger to his lips, and they shared a secret glance at Mum who was fussing over Caroline.

Denis raised the bottle and sipped. He spluttered and coughed, and Dad rubbed his back.

"What's gotten into you?" Mum asked, turning back to them.

Trying to suppress his laughter, Dad said, "Nothing. Just a fishbone." He winked at Denis. Later, when he was putting him to bed, Dad said, "You'll get used to it, lad. Belgium beers are the best. You'll learn that when you're older."

Denis looked at the beer bottle in his hand as Oliver pulled a chair close to him. The label said it was Japanese.

When Oliver spoke, his voice was soft. "Did you sneak on the train, or do you really have a ticket?"

"How do I get a ticket that gives me an entire carriage to myself?"

"That's not an answer."

Denis shrugged and faced the window.

"All right. Annabelle, call the inspector back, will you?"

"No," Denis said. "Look. Fine. I snuck on. But I'm friends with one of the engineers. Just let me off at the next stop and give me your PayPal. I'll transfer you the ticket cost."

To the barman, Oliver said, "What's the next stop?"

"Newry, sir."

"Perfect," Denis said. "I've never been to Newry. It'll be fun."

Annabelle hovered by the door. "Am I getting him or not?"

Although he didn't look up, Denis guessed Oliver shook his head, because Annabelle never left.

"Are you in some kind of trouble?" Oliver asked.

"Are you some kind of detective?"

"Denis, I'm trying to help you, here."

Denis pulled the pocket square out and waved it. "You already did, thanks." He pushed it back into his pocket in case Oliver decided he wanted it back. There was no reason for him to keep it, but he didn't want to let it go.

"Well. It's a long way to Newry in the world's slowest train. You'd better get comfortable."

Oliver went to the bar and spoke with Annabelle out of Denis' earshot. From her mannerisms, he guessed she wasn't agreeing with whatever he was saying.

Denis watched his own reflection in the window and drank from his beer. Lloyd—that was Oliver's last name. It struck him as Oliver walked away.

Oliver Lloyd. The son of the newspaper owner. Famous for being rich and probably very little else. Bit of a partygoer. And full of self-importance. But sexy in a way that meant Denis could never look at him directly. If attractive men didn't have faces, it'd be much better. Denis could stare and the man would be none the wiser. He was imagining Oliver without his shirt, wondering what his skin felt like.

He wished he was back in the luggage car, pressed between a suitcase and Tom's strong arm. Tom had held Denis' lifelong attraction, but Oliver Lloyd made his stomach hurt.

He finished his beer and pressed his forehead to the cold glass of the window. It vibrated as the train stumbled through the dark countryside. He didn't know what he was going to do next. Oliver would see him off the train at Newry and he didn't have any Northern Irish banknotes.

Calling his mum was out of the question. He looked at his phone. It was just after ten o'clock. He could call Caroline, but he'd have to wait until the train passed through a town or city because he didn't have any signal right now. Caroline would transfer him some money. He couldn't expect much but she'd give him enough to get home.

Thinking about her made him wonder if she'd

managed to placate their mum. He left in such a hurry that he hadn't considered the repercussions or how it would affect his sister. It wasn't her fight to have. He should never have left. But the truth was that he was scared of their mother and what she would tell their neighbours. "Denis is queer now. He likes putting his thing in other men."

And Caroline didn't deserve to be left to mop up after Denis' confession. He still didn't know what possessed him to blurt those words out. "I think I'm gay."

He couldn't even be honest with her. *I think I'm gay.* Like he wasn't sure.

But damn he was certain about it when he glanced at Oliver by the bar. Oliver Lloyd. Famous for being rich. And sexy as all hell.

8.

OLIVER

Oliver was trying to listen to Annabelle, but his attention kept drifting back to Denis. There was something about his eyes that made Oliver want to pull him into his arms and hold tight until the world crumbled away in a cloud of dust.

He was drawn to him, which he knew was stupid. He was always drawn to the bad-boy image. Maybe it was the hoodie and the sagging jeans. Maybe it was the angry expression on Denis' face, or the permanency of his sadness, that attracted him. Sad and angry was Oliver's type. But if he hadn't learned his lesson after Walt, maybe he never would.

He looked at him, sitting in an oversized crushed-velvet chair, nursing a beer and staring out the window, and he wanted to pull his hood down and get a good look at his face. He wanted to study every detail so that he could recall it later when he was alone in his room, naked under the covers of his bed.

He guessed Denis was around nineteen or twenty, but the soul behind his eyes was vast and ancient. Those eyes hid something, though. Inside him, buried underneath the angry words and sarcasm, Oliver knew there was a melancholy that was too raw to be acknowledged.

"Are you listening?"

Oliver tore his glance from Denis and turned to Annabelle. "What?"

"I said we should have left him with the ticket inspector and never got involved."

"What if that was me back there without a ticket?"

"You wouldn't be so stupid."

"Well, he's here now. He's our responsibility."

"No, he isn't. He's only our responsibility because you made him. What're you going to do with him?"

"What do you mean, 'Do with him'?"

"You have a walkthrough at midnight. And I don't want him sitting there messing with the train's feng shui."

"Centre your ch'i, Belle. He's here and I won't throw him out."

"It's a long way to Newry. What if he murders us before we get there?"

Oliver gave a nod to the barman and said, "Adam, tell my P.A. that he doesn't look like a murderer."

Twisting the cap off a glass bottle of water, Adam said, "I don't know if murderers have a particular look about their faces, but that kid looks far too sad to be violent."

"You," Annabelle said, "need to remain impartial. You're not allowed to take his side."

"I'm not taking sides. I'm just stating facts."

Annabelle returned her attention to her iPad. If anybody could scroll through Facebook with an angry finger, it was her.

Oliver took his sparkling water and turned. He wanted to sit in front of Denis and stare at him with open admiration. But that sort of thing normally ends in a fistfight or a court case. What he really wanted was to ask Denis to take a walk with him. But they were on a train with nowhere to walk to.

He wanted to touch him inside—and not in a spiritual way.

But before he took a step towards him, Annabelle said, "Ollie, please."

"What?"

"I know what you're thinking."

"You definitely don't," Oliver said, and he could feel his cheeks flush. If she knew what he was imagining, she'd quit her job and walk home from here.

"I saw his sad face, too. He's going through some shit and it's not your place to fix him."

"I don't want to fix him." But he did. That's exactly what he wanted to do. After the sex stuff.

"Ollie, we've got another six hours on this train. Don't do anything stupid. Let him sulk and when we get to Newry, we'll hand him over to the ticket inspector. He's not a kid, he can make his own way home."

"I'm not handing him over to anyone, Belle. Look at him. He's carrying something heavy. What kind of ass would I be if I let him carry it alone?"

"Whatever baggage he's got is not your concern. You can't save the whole world."

"Yes, you can," Oliver said. "You just do it one person at a time."

He walked with purpose towards the sadness.

Denis didn't turn from the window, but when their eyes locked in the reflection, Oliver held his gaze as long as he could. Even in the dark mirror image, Denis' eyes were trenches into a lifetime of loneliness.

"All right?"

Denis shrugged. The way he had wrapped both hands around the beer bottle, Oliver couldn't tell if it was empty or untouched.

"Look. I'm not here to give you a hard time, okay? What happened out there—forget it. I don't care if you have a ticket. What matters is that you're here, in my carriage, and I had to lie to a ticket inspector in order to make that happen."

"I didn't ask you to do that."

Oliver sat in the chair opposite Denis and didn't speak until Denis faced him. It was a trick he'd learned from his father. If you want somebody's attention, stop talking.

"I did what I thought was right at the time. It's not my place to judge, but you look as though you need the help. Do you?"

"Do I what?"

"Need help?"

Denis looked at his beer bottle before taking a drink. "I'm not a charity case."

"That's not what I asked."

"No. I don't need your help."

Maybe I need yours, Oliver wanted to say. Instead, he changed his tactics. "You really don't know who I am?"

"Should I?"

"Honestly, I hope you don't. I'm sick of having conversations with people who only want one thing—my money."

"Mr Money-Bags over here." Denis' words were layered with sarcasm. But in true style, Oliver wasn't sure if it was friendly banter or outright distaste. In Ireland, the two sounded the same.

"I wasn't boasting," Oliver pointed out. Denis didn't respond. "What's in Belfast that made you sneak onto an overnight train that's going two and a half kilometres an hour? It's like you want to go someplace but don't want to arrive."

"I didn't know the damn thing would be moving so slow. We'd get there quicker if we got out and walked."

The fact that Denis said *we* didn't go unnoticed. Oliver's mind twisted with wickedness. He pushed the thought away. "Yeah, but then we wouldn't have the pleasure of Annabelle's company."

Denis looked across the carriage at his P.A. "Is she always so angry?"

"She's not angry, she's just protective."

"I kind of felt like she wanted to carry me up the side of the Empire State Building."

It took Oliver a second to understand what Denis meant, and then he laughed hard enough to make Annabelle scowl at him.

"She's never given me King Kong vibes, but yeah, she's not someone you want to cross."

Denis smiled, and when he did Oliver's chest tightened. But Denis flattened his lips and his face returned to its neutral sadness.

"Denis?" Oliver said, forcing the word into a question, making him look at him again. When he did, heat spread across Oliver's cheeks. "I'm a good listener. If you want to talk."

Denis sipped from his beer and stared out the window. "How many kilometres to Newry?"

"You don't have to get off at Newry. If you need to get to Belfast, you might as well stay on the train."

"I wouldn't want to be a burden to you."

"For God's sake, Denis. I'm offering you a hand. You don't have to bite it."

"I told you. I don't need your charity."

"It's not charity. You're already on the train—why bother getting off before you need to, just to make a point?"

Denis drank his beer until the bottle was empty and he placed it on the table. He stuffed his hands back into his pockets and Oliver could tell he was chewing the inside of his cheek.

"Fine. Okay. Come on. Follow me." Oliver stood and gave Denis' shoe a gentle kick.

"What—you're handing me in now?"

"I just said I was trying to help you. Why would I go back on that and turn you in?" he walked towards the end of the carriage. "Are you coming?"

He didn't turn back to check if Denis was following him. He opened a door to one of the cabins and entered. If Denis didn't come in behind him, he'd look stupid.

And then he saw his shadow inch across the carpet and his face appear at the open doorway.

"You can have this room. There's a bed, a window, and a shower through there if you want."

"Are you saying I stink?"

"I'm saying you can do whatever the hell you want, Denis. Shower. Don't shower. I couldn't care less. Sleep in the bed or stick your head out the window. I'm not going to hand you over to the inspectors, but if you're going to sulk, you might as well do it in here where I don't have to look at the anger on your face." He stepped out of the room and gripped the door handle. "I have to do a walkthrough of the train later—the joys of being such a rich bastard on a train full of snot-nosed teen-age girls. The last thing I need is you being judgemental, too."

When he closed the door and went back to the bar, Annabelle raised her gaze to him. He could hear the question without her asking.

"I don't want to hear it, Belle." To Adam, he asked, "How soon do we get to Newry?"

He always fell for the wrong type. Pick a bad boy, any bad boy. They'll break your heart as quick as your bedsprings.

9.

DENIS

enis threw himself on the bed with a groan. He pulled the pillow from under him and held it against his face in frustration. He didn't mean to be judgemental, as Oliver called him. He just had issues—family matters, as well as an enormous fear of talking to attractive men.

He was never one for socialising much. With a small group of close friends, Denis didn't really know what it was like to be popular. He was middle-of-the-road in every sense, and that suited him fine. He kept his hair short, his clothes muted, and his voice low. He didn't consider himself much to look at—average height, average build.

He was just average.

So, when a gorgeous man spoke to him, Denis' tongue would tie itself in knots and refuse to unravel until he was alone again. He didn't even have to fancy the guy, it just had to be someone lower down the Ugly Tree than him. The fact that Tom had convinced him to get on a train when Denis was attempting to throw himself off a bridge was a testament to Denis' inability to speak up around attractive men.

He wished his dad was still alive to talk him through these awkward situations. Dad always had an opinion on everything, and a solution to go with each problem. "Don't squeeze the brakes too hard when they're wet or you'll go over the handlebars, son." Dad wouldn't have thrown him out for being gay.

He never gave it much thought before, but the day after his father's funeral was when he began to fall away from his mother. When they had found his note, she refused to let Denis read it. "It's not for you. He was my husband." When they pulled his body from the lough, she did not let him see it. And when they lowered him into the ground, she held him tight, his face against her long black coat, and would not let him look at the coffin on its final descent.

She didn't cry. Not at first.

But Denis did, and she was too spaced out to comfort him. He knew, even at eight years old, that her grief at losing her husband had turned her into a zombie. But who was going to hold him in his grief?

The morning after the funeral, Denis knocked on his

parent's bedroom door and saw that she was still wearing her black dress from the day before. She sat on the edge of the bed—Dad's side—and stared at the wall. It hadn't occurred to him at the time that she had been sitting there since yesterday, unable to move.

"Mammy?"

The only indication that she was alive was the rise and fall of her shoulders as she breathed.

"Mammy."

Denis saw his father's personal effects on the dresser. They were returned by a policeman three days ago, a few clear plastic bags containing his clothes, wallet, one shoelace, and a separate bag that held his father's suicide note.

Denis shouldn't have done it, but he couldn't stop himself. He lifted the small bag, closed the door, and went to his room. Caroline was playing with her dolls on the landing.

He unsealed the evidence and shook it so that the crumpled envelope fell onto his bed. He was reluctant to touch it, knowing his father had held it recently. He thought he could smell him on it.

When he unfolded it, he closed his eyes. Would it matter what kind of apology Dad gave for taking his life? There were no words that could bring him back.

Denis opened his eyes. There was no note inside it, and the back of the envelope had three words scrawled across it.

You did this.

That was the day Denis stopped crying. He slipped the envelope back into the plastic bag, thumbed the seal closed, and put it back on his mother's dresser while she sat on the bed, oblivious.

Thinking back on that day, Denis wasn't sure who the note was meant for. He assumed the *you* was his mother. But the note didn't say, *Dear Jennifer*. Maybe Denis was at fault. Or his father's boss. Or a neighbour. Dad wasn't here to tell him who.

And he wasn't around to offer any words of wisdom about Oliver.

Denis wanted to apologise and start over, but he knew that wasn't an option. No matter how hard you try, you can't take back your words.

When his phone vibrated in his pocket, it startled him. He'd been without a phone signal since getting on this damn train.

He heard the sigh in Caroline's voice when he answered. "Hey, sis."

"Where are you? I've been trying to get through for an hour."

"I'm on a train. Where's Mum?"

"In her room. Where are you going?"

Denis sat up, elbows on his knees, and looked at the darkness outside the window. "I don't know. I'll be back tomorrow. Are you all right?"

"She's not screaming and crying anymore."

Denis didn't speak. He offered Caroline his silence as comfort.

"I've told her you're still you. That you haven't changed."

Maybe that was the problem. "She knows that, Car. I don't even think it's the gay thing. She's just angry all the time."

"You and Mammy, you're just the same."

"I'm nothing like her. What did she say when I left?"

"Who knows? She was screaming that much she made herself hoarse. By the time she calmed down, she wasn't making much sense. But she called you worse than Dad." Caroline lowered her voice. "I can hear her moving around upstairs."

"Are you going to be okay without me for the night?"

"I'm not the gay one, Denny. She's not angry with me."

"She's not upset you're sticking up for me?"

"Of course, she is. But she knows I'm straight. I can still give her babies."

"I can give her babies, too."

"Yeah, from a test tube."

"Shut up."

"Make me."

Denis smiled. He didn't know how he would have survived without her. When Dad was gone, and Mum was gone, too, even if her body was still there, Denis imposed all his attention on Caroline. He brushed the knots from her hair and helped her into her maroon uniform for junior infants' school, and he poured the milk into her cereal, obliging her when she said, "More,

90

more," and pouring her a fresh bowl when she said it was too soggy.

He pinned posters on the walls and helped her learn her numbers while Mum shuffled around the house like a ghost. And when Mum forgot to pick her up from school in the coming years, which happened more often as they got older, Denis was the one who raced to the primary school and held her hand as they waited for the bus.

In return, Caroline was there for him when he fractured his elbow at thirteen. She wrapped his arm in a scarf and sat with him in A&E for three hours while Mum was at work.

Their mother wasn't always a zombie. Six months after Dad's funeral, she got a new job, and only drank in the evenings. She learned to drive—that was always Dad's job—and she made dinner and cleaned their rooms. And sometimes she laughed with them, just like old times.

But Denis never forgave her.

You did this.

"Are you there?" Caroline asked. Her voice was distant and broken.

"Car? Caroline?" But the line went dead.

He sent her a text that said he'd lost his signal and would call her in the morning, and he stared at the indicator below his message. *Not sent.*

She'd get it when his phone picked up a network again.

Denis looked around the small cabin and flinched when a train on the opposite track rattled the window and stole the air from the room for a split second. Even though it was dark outside, the room darkened as the train sped by.

He flicked the switch in the small bathroom and a series of wall lights illuminated the shower, a toilet, and the rack of thick white towels. He pushed a button on the wall and the shower sparked to life. The water was warm and soft on his fingers. He didn't intend to take a shower, but he was undressed and standing under its decadent stream of needles before he realised what he was doing. He closed his eyes and let the water beat his face.

The complimentary shampoo and shower gels smelled like watermelon, and when he was done, he wrapped himself in an oversized towel with the train's logo in one corner, and he sat on the bed and stared at the passing night. A chill itched at his bare shoulders.

As he was getting dressed, there was a knock at the door. With his jeans on and his hoodie in his hands, Denis said, "Yeah?"

Oliver opened the door, cleared his throat, and said, "We're ordering food. Are you hungry?"

Denis pulled the hoodie over his head and smiled. His hair was damp, and he brushed his fingers through it. "Sure. I'll be there in a second." When his host was closing the door, he added, "Oliver?"

Oliver looked at him.

He hesitated. He didn't know what he was going to say. I took a shower like you told me. I'm a mess inside and I shouldn't take it out on you. Instead, he said, "Thanks."

Oliver closed the door.

Denis looked at his phone. His message to Caroline had gone through and her reply was unread. *Be good. See you tomorrow, butt bandit.*

10.

OLIVER

When Denis came out of his cabin, Oliver was studying the dinner menu. He made a point of not looking up. He hadn't expected to see Denis shirtless and couldn't shake the image from his mind. He was slim but not skinny, and apart from two small round moles on his upper chest, his skin was ivory and flawless. There was a hint of hair below his navel, a thin trail that etched a dark path into the waistband of his jeans, and the Adonis-belt grooves of his lower abdomen accentuated the tautness of his stomach.

Oliver read the words on the menu but couldn't think of eating anything other than Denis.

Annabelle held a menu out to their guest. "Are you two going to play nice, this time?"

"Yes, Mum," Oliver said.

Denis grimaced and took the laminated card.

When Oliver convinced his body to turn from the bar to Denis, he said, "The linguine looks good. Unless you've filled up on vol-au-vents." He meant it as a joke, but the strained look on Denis' face made him turn away.

"Linguine sounds good," Denis said, handing the menu back. He didn't even look at it.

Oliver nodded to Adam who used the phone behind the bar to call their order through. "Can I get you another drink while you wait?"

"I'm buying," Denis said as he took a stool far enough away from the others to make Oliver feel as though he didn't want to be there.

"It's an open bar," Adam said.

"That's what I was hoping." He turned to Oliver. His smile was thin and shy. Oliver wondered how soft his lips were. "Beer? Or are you a martini kind of guy?"

"I'm a teetotal kind of guy." To Adam, he said, "Sparkling water, please."

Denis appeared to give it some thought, then ordered a lager.

Oliver shouldn't have taken it as a kick in the teeth, adding insult to the injury of having to sit with a non-drinker, but as Denis took his first mouthful of beer, he looked altogether satisfied with his choice.

Annabelle ordered a lime and soda.

And Oliver's gaze lowered to the marble-effect countertop.

The train rocked. Oliver concentrated on the repetitive laughter of the wheels on the track. Modern trains seemed to hum as they glided over the railway lines. The difference was as striking as tabloids and broadsheets, in the same way that his electric car whirred with silent efficiency compared to the racket of an older petrol or diesel car. He knew the former was better for the environment, but he missed the noise of the latter. Just as he loved the noise of the old hydraulics on this steam engine.

The instrumental jazz that floated from the hidden speakers above the bar made his fingertips dance across the counter, but he shook his wrist to lose the rhythm and hide his love for elevator music. Not that Denis was even looking.

From the corner of his eye, Oliver saw that Denis was picking at the label of his beer bottle. Thin curls of torn paper littered the bar in front of him. If they were sitting a little closer, it would feel like an awkward first date.

Oliver knew all about those. When he was seventeen, he joined a dating app. He didn't use his real name and his profile photo was of his torso. When he spoke to someone who seemed normal, he kept their friendship online for a few weeks to make sure it was worth it. When the guy asked to meet him—for drinks, he stressed, but Oliver knew what drinks led to—he agreed. He dressed lowkey and wore a hat, and when they met, the guy recognised him. He went from being full of bravado and innuendo by text message, to shy and stuttering his words.

Drinks, that day, did not lead to anything more. And Oliver removed the app from his phone.

When there was a chime from the carriage door, Adam let the waiters in. One of the men wheeled a trolley with their meals, while another laid their flatware on one of the round tables.

Annabelle's iPad was jacked into a wall outlet at the bar as she scrolled through it, and so she took her gourmet vegan burger back to her stool.

Denis sat at the table and waited for Oliver to join him before twisting some linguine onto his fork. Oliver killed the *Lady and the Tramp* vibes his brain had conjured.

They ate in silence, except for the erotic noises coming from Annabelle whose burger was evidently working all kinds of magic in her mouth. Oliver noticed Denis glance at her, and he smiled and put a finger to his lips. "Every time," he whispered. "I wish a vegan burger could do that for me."

Denis chuckled around a mouthful of pasta before coughing the smile away. Oliver saw how his face dropped, as though he'd just remembered he was an angry scally whose only facial expression was a permanent scowl.

The rest of their meal was swallowed in silence.

When Adam took their empty plates, Denis knocked back the last of his beer and stood.

Oliver said, "You're not confined to your room, Denis.

You can stay here. Have another drink."

Denis slouched back into his chair and Adam brought another round. Oliver could have kicked himself. He wanted Denis close so that he could look at him with carefully disguised longing, but the awkward silence was thinning the air.

Eat your heart out, Mount Everest. Denis' sulking demeanour was a bigger hill to climb.

"You still haven't told me anything about yourself," Oliver said.

"What do you want to know?"

"Anything." What he wanted to say was *everything*. "Who is Denis—I'm sorry, I don't even know your last name."

"Murphy."

"Good Irish name."

"Where's Lloyd from?"

"It's Welsh, I think. Do you want to tell me why you snuck on a train now?"

"Why don't you tell me why you're here," Denis said. "It can't be for the media attention."

Oliver nodded with vigour. "Paparazzi are clinging to the side of the train."

"Must be freezing for them."

"If a few of them get frostbite, I'm not going to complain." When it felt as though the conversation was ending, Oliver took a deep breath. "You really want to know why I'm here?"

Denis shrugged, but he leaned closer, his elbows on

the table.

"I'm not sure how much you know about me."

"Very little."

It didn't sound like he meant it as an insult. Oliver said, "I've had some wild times. I used to be known as a bit of a lager lout. Anyway. One bad relationship too many and I checked myself into rehab. I'm six months sober. And my family couldn't care less. They're too wrapped up in their own issues. I think my mum is a borderline alcoholic; sometimes I forget what my dad looks like, he's away so often; and I'm pretty certain my sister wants to divorce her husband and shack up with the gardener."

"That sucks."

"The only good thing in my life is my four-year-old niece whose birthday is coming up and she's far too young to realise how much of a stuck-up narcissist her mother is. Which I guess is a very long-winded way of telling you I'm on this train because my family are a pain in the ass and don't even get me started on my so-called friends, who have their hands deeper in my pockets than I do. I just needed one night away from them."

Telling Denis his story felt cathartic. He leaned back in his chair and studied his glass as the sparkling water ebbed in time with the swaying of the train carriage.

Their eyes locked for a second longer than was comfortable, and Oliver saw that Denis felt his pain.

"It seems to me that you're here for similar reasons," Oliver said. "I guess you needed to clear your head, too?"

"Something like that." Denis stood up, taking his empty beer bottle to the bar, and Oliver watched as he ordered another. He crossed to the row of cabins before turning back. "Thanks for dinner."

When he disappeared into his room, Oliver was perplexed. He had opened up to him and was expecting some reciprocating conversation.

"Is he for real?" he asked Annabelle, crossing to the bar. "You tell a man your life sucks and all he says is, 'Thanks for dinner.'"

Annabelle stroked his arm when he took the stool beside her. "He's not ready to talk yet. Let him stew in his room for a while."

"I don't know what to do."

"Do nothing. It's not your job to fix everyone, Ollie. You know that. If he wants to tell you why he's running away from his problems, he will. Just leave him be."

"I wish he'd relax around us. We're not the cops."

"Want me to steal his phone?"

"What?"

"I don't mind calling his mum and giving her what for."

"He's not a kid, Belle."

"No? Then stop treating him like one. He'll open up to you in time, or he'll get off the train in the morning without saying another word. Either way, it's not like you're ever going to see him again."

But that was Oliver's issue. He wanted to see him again. More than anything, he wanted to see him naked.

He asked Adam for another glass of water before his arousal became evident. And then he took his drink back to the table to sulk.

11.

DENIS

What an idiot. Oliver told him he was teetotal, and Denis ordered a beer. Smooth. That'll win him the Nobel Prize for Intellect. It was like asking somebody how their mother was—at their mother's funeral.

He closed the door of his cabin and put his beer bottle on the nightstand. It foamed as the train pitched on a corner, and he tried to catch it, but whatever gaping yaw the train had stumbled over made him take a step forward and steady himself. It was momentary—a wobble, nothing more—but it made his heart claw its way into his throat.

The beer toppled but he caught it before it fell off the nightstand. It was a sign. Drinking beer in the company of a sober guy was damn rude.

He drank from the bottle, glancing at the door to make sure he wasn't being watched. When Oliver told him he was teetotal, Denis didn't ask for a beer out of spite. He did it to mask his nerves. Alcohol softened the edges of his busy mind and made him slow down enough to relax. He was never tested for ADHD, but his mum swore blind he was dipped in crazy cream at birth. Alcohol mellowed him. So did grass, but it messed with his head too much, so he didn't smoke it often.

Denis would get drunk just to stop the noise. Fat lot of good it was doing him around Oliver, though. When the fit celebrity opened his mouth, there was too much noise to listen. The world was a distraction from Oliver Lloyd.

His lifelong attraction to Tom McInnis was dwindling. Tom had been the only attractive guy in Clannon Village, someone Denis could fixate on for years. Even when he was thirteen and Tom was flunking out of his Junior Cert year, any chance to spend time in his company was enough. He swore that Tom was the only reason he and Aaron had remained friends for so long.

Denis once deliberately broke the chain on his bike, two days after Tom had fixed it, and he wheeled it up to Tom's yard and gave a shy smile when Tom said, "What the hell have you done to it? It looks mangled."

"Can you fix it?"

"You know me, Denny. I can fix anything."

But Tom couldn't fix Denis' feelings towards Oliver. Oliver wasn't a grease monkey like Tom. He didn't fit into Denis' social circle. And yet there was a magnetic force that pulled at him. Oliver's charm was his openness.

During dinner, Oliver had revealed something about himself that Denis didn't think was possible. He was a rich star who had problems like anyone else.

Money wasn't the cure.

"One bad relationship too many," Oliver had said. Denis noted there were no pronouns involved in that sentence. Some distant memory of a half-forgotten TV interview made him think Oliver was gay, but he couldn't be certain. And his gaydar was broken. He hated himself for not paying attention to celebrity culture.

He wanted to ask him. That's what brave people did. They didn't hide in their room and wonder; they asked.

"You gay?"

"Yeah. You?"

"Yeah. Want to slip out of your clothes?"

"Sure."

But life was never that simple. He went to a gay bar once. Or, rather, he hovered outside a gay bar until some old guy with a grey beard asked him if he wanted to share a kebab—he wasn't holding a kebab, so Denis didn't know if it was a euphemism—and then he scarpered across town to a straight bar and played pinball and drank pints until he puked. Like a real man.

He slapped his forehead and sat on the bed. He realised how much internal homophobia he had and hated himself for it. Why couldn't he be open about who he was? Tom had spent the evening talking to him about girls and Denis hadn't corrected him. He could never truly be accepting of love until he accepted himself. Sure, he'd love to share a bed with another man but, like Simon Peter, he'd deny it three times in the morning. He thanked his mum for that guilt.

She wasn't religious but was happy to call on Padre Pio when it suited her. The last time Denis went to mass was when he was fourteen. It was Easter Sunday and Mum was dating a guy who insisted they attend as a family. He took Denis shopping on the Thursday after school and bought him a suit, all grey tweed and cream buttons.

Denis was forced to sit beside him on the hard church pew, and when his restless leg syndrome drove his knee into a bouncing mosh pit dance, Gregg put his hand on his leg to stop it.

"Sit at peace," Gregg whispered, "or I'll cut your fucking leg off."

"We're over," Mum said, right there in the chapel. "You don't threaten my children." And that was the last time they saw Gregg. And the last time Denis was inside a church.

Mum continued to go on a semi-regular basis. She made a point of attending the same church after her breakup with Gregg, and Denis guessed he never showed his face again.

In time, she stopped going. The holy images of Jesus and Mary still hung on their walls, and there was a hard-cover bible on the coffee table in the living room, but it was an ornament that was never touched—except that one time Caroline used it to kill a spider. Denis wondered if her sacrilege would earn her a seat near the gays in hell.

He avoided religion. Not because he didn't believe in a higher power, but because organised religion was made up of ten per cent believers, and ninety per cent vicious liars. How could he believe in a God who didn't believe in him? How could God prefer Gregg singing his praises than Denis?

He looked at his beer bottle. It was almost empty. He wanted another but didn't dare go and ask for one.

He wondered how easy it would be to let Oliver know he was gay. He couldn't slip it into conversation without pointing out that his mother kicked him out three hours ago. He was so close to throwing himself off a bridge before Tom convinced him to get on a train— the very train where he'd met Oliver. Life is like that—if you get through the day without killing yourself, something wonderful happens.

But Oliver was so far out of his league. Denis was from an under 21s grassroots home club while Oliver was FA Cup. Their lives were as different as fish fingers and oysters. Denis' claim to fame was being in the audience of *The Late Late Toy Show* one Christmas when he was five. Oliver Lloyd was outright famous.

It would never work. And yet, all he wanted to do was fold himself into Oliver's embrace and stay there until the world stopped turning.

He didn't know if his dad felt the same about his mum when they first met. He imagined red roses and bad poetry. *I love thee like a duck loves muck.*

With his beer empty, Denis lay on the bed, his hands behind his head and an ache in his chest. It seemed family drama happened in all corners of the world. Until Oliver told him about his absent father, alcoholic mother and wayward sister, Denis assumed he had a perfect life. Oliver should have been the kind of guy who sat in the backseat of a Rolls Royce, sipping champagne and eating caviar without a care in the world. He should have men and women draped over his arms and laughter in his heart. Rich folk can have somebody on staff to fix their hair and wipe their ass, but money can't fix a broken family.

Maybe the only thing separating Oliver Lloyd from Denis Murphy was a couple of fat zeros in the bank.

The public address system chimed, and a garbled voice said, "We will shortly be journeying through Drogheda. Please note, *The Duchess of Dublin*'s next stop is Newry. We will not be stopping at Drogheda. I would like to remind you that Oliver Lloyd will be walking through the train to greet our guests in thirty minutes. That's thirty minutes until Oliver Lloyd's walkthrough. On behalf of myself and *The Duchess of Dublin*, I would like to thank you for travelling with us, and don't forget to avail yourselves of the gift shop in Carriages C and G where you will find twenty-five per cent off selected items."

The man listed some things for sale, including a scale model of *The Duchess of Dublin* priced at only £200. Denis was upset he didn't have enough money in the bank, or he'd want to buy twelve—one for each mantelpiece in his mansion.

He sat up. If Oliver was going to walk through the train and wave like the Queen of England, Denis wanted to watch. Let's see the rich kid do rich kid things.

12.

OLIVER

"**A**bsolutely not."

"You can't keep me cooped up in here."

"Let him come if he wants to."

"Not a chance." Annabelle shook her head as she put her fists on her hips in a power pose. "It's bad enough you're going to get mobbed from one end of the train to the other. I don't want to be responsible for him, too."

"I can look after myself."

"It's my walkthrough," Oliver said. "Let me settle this. Denis, do you promise not to blow the train up and make Annabelle look bad?"

"I'll do my best."

"Annabelle, do you promise not to clip Denis round the ear if he steps out of line?"

"Why do you go through your life making a joke out of everything?"

"Because the world's too miserable to add another bleeding heart to it. Answer the question."

Annabelle scowled. "I'll do my best," she mocked Denis' words.

Oliver shook his head. He shared a glance with Adam that said, I know I'm six months sober, but I'll probably need a double vodka when this is over. For a while, he missed the hangovers as well as the partying. Waking up at twenty to five in the morning—every morning—when the alcohol wore off and the hangover kicked in was his standby routine. It got to the point where he didn't need to look at the clock, he woke at the same time each day with alcoholic fervour.

At the time, he hated the tired wakefulness. But in his first few months of sobriety, he woke at confusing times of the morning—normal times when normal people woke—and he missed those early morning headaches. It freaked him out until he learned to love a Sunday morning lie-in. He would stretch and yawn and turn over as the morning sunlight waded into his room through the open blinds, and he'd lie there in a blissful, well-rested fog of slumber.

But he reminded himself that most people weren't teetotal. And that wasn't an issue. They had a right to drink and enjoy themselves, Denis included.

With five minutes until showdown, there was a knock on the carriage door and a train representative entered. The voice on the public address system said, "We remind our passengers that Oliver Lloyd will be enjoying a walk through the cars in five minutes. Mr Lloyd's agents request that passengers please remain seated unless advised otherwise by management."

"Mr Lloyd's agents?" Oliver asked Annabelle.

She shrugged. "Double-oh-Seven ain't got nothing on me. If you get taken down by a sex-starved grandmother who's had a hip replacement and one too many vitamin pills, I'm not going to be held responsible."

"I absolve you of all responsibility."

"I'll have that in writing, please."

Denis said, "If you two don't stop bickering, I'd say you were both a pair of grandmothers."

Annabelle nudged Oliver's shoulder. "Look at that. The kid's got balls after all."

Oliver smiled at Denis. He still wasn't sure how to approach him and his brooding mannerisms. When they lined up at the door in advance of the clock striking midnight, Oliver breathed in as Denis stepped behind him. He smelled like watermelon.

Oliver's nerves were on edge. Public appearances were one thing but doing it on a train—no matter how slow it was moving—meant he had nowhere to escape if one of his fans got out of hand. It wouldn't be the first time it had happened. He opened a new shopping centre in Limerick a few years before and mall security had to wrestle a guy to the ground when he got too close. "I love you, Ollie," the man shouted. The sexual filth that spouted from his lips was enough to make even a seasoned hooker blush.

Denis said, "I feel like I'm waiting in line for a shot from the school nurse."

"Was your school nurse as gruff as mine? Four-day stubble and hairy knuckles?" Oliver asked, and he was grateful for the interruption in his thoughts.

"Turn your head and cough."

Oliver laughed like he hadn't in a long time. Annabelle shushed them.

"I swear you're a pair of unruly schoolboys."

Denis turned his head and coughed.

They laughed harder.

The train representative checked her watch and said, "Are you ready, Mr Lloyd?"

He inhaled, holding his tongue to the roof of his mouth for six seconds before releasing it, and he nodded.

"Time to work your magic," Denis said.

"If it looks like I'm drowning in a sea of people, will you rescue me?"

"No," Denis said, but he was smiling.

Oliver strode into the next car and a cheer erupted from the passengers. The girl who had spoken to him at the bar earlier blushed when he smiled at her. "I'm so sorry for asking you the time, Oliver. I'm mortified."

"Don't be. It's all good." He signed her dress with a Sharpie when she asked him to and posed for a selfie with her and her friend.

"How much money have you in your pockets, right

112

now?" one teenage lad said.

Oliver winked. "I don't carry cash, I'm Oliver Lloyd." The lad shook his hand.

Oliver preferred dealing with men over women. Girls swooned and blushed and screamed, but guys, especially the straight ones, went out of their way to act normal around him like they had something to prove. Girls wanted to bed him, but straight boys just wanted to have a pint with him. Maybe they thought they would have girls throwing themselves at them too, by association.

Annabelle waved him forward. She walked a few paces ahead, controlling the crowd. She might be small, but she was mighty. She came across as acerbic more often than not, but she was his best friend. She was used to battling people off—with her fists on occasion—and she found it difficult to switch off the security alarm in her brain that must be screaming at her with everyone who approached him. He hoped Denis could see that she wasn't being mean when she spoke to him, she was just being protective.

He looked around for Denis but couldn't see him. He thought maybe he'd run off at the first opportunity, but then he spotted him on a stool by the bar. His eyes followed Oliver around the carriage like a painting. He gave a small wave of his hand.

"Oh my God, I love you, Oliver," a small voice said. When Oliver turned his attention away from Denis, he saw a girl of about ten or eleven years old. She wore an oversized T-shirt with Oliver's face on it, and her cheeks were flushed. She hid behind her mother in a shy manner.

"Woah, I love the T-shirt. What's your name?" Oliver crouched down to her level and coaxed her forward.

"Jamie," the girl said, and she flattened her lips as though she'd spoken out of turn.

"Do you have something for me to sign, Jamie?"

The girl's mother said, "Her room is filled with your posters and toys. And she's asked Santa for your biography."

Oliver smiled. "It's only an unofficial biography, so don't believe everything you read, okay?"

He signed Jamie's T-shirt, right over his own face, and she said, "Can I kiss you?"

He grinned and offered her his cheek. Jamie leaned in, planted a kiss on him, and whispered, "I'm trans."

Oliver knew when to make a song and dance about something and when to play it down. His smile was wide and warm. "Can I kiss *you*?"

Jamie nodded but before leaning in, Oliver glanced at her mother for permission. When she gave her consent, Oliver kissed Jamie's cheek and whispered, "Thank you for telling me."

"I told him," he heard her say to her mum as they stepped away.

Oliver looked back at the bar and saw Denis watching him. Jamie told him that she was a trans girl with such wondrous ease that he questioned why he hadn't told Denis he was gay. He wasn't sure if he was scared of rejection or scared of the subsequent heartache that would ultimately follow his admission.

It appeared Denis truly had no idea who Oliver Lloyd was or, more to the point, didn't care. Oliver liked that his wealth was irrelevant when they spoke. When his walkthrough was complete, he'd make a conscious effort to connect with the brooding stranger and maybe, by the time they stepped off the train in Belfast, he'd have a friend if nothing more. He'd stop looking for love. Someone who didn't want him for the size of his wallet would be enough. They had shared a laugh, before his walkthrough, and Oliver was convinced there was a germ of something akin to understanding or respect. It seemed Denis was warming to him.

"This way," Annabelle said.

Oliver smiled and nodded and answered the same old questions he was always asked in these situations. Just once he wanted someone to ask him what his favourite book was, not where he bought his shoes.

"I made you a casserole," a woman said, holding out a dish wrapped in a chequered tea towel. "I read online that beef casserole was your favourite."

"Thank you," Oliver smiled, taking the plate and handing it to Annabelle. He never ate the food he was given by strangers. His brain conjured up too many horror stories of being poisoned or ingesting enough sleeping pills to knock him out and he'd wake up in a motel bathroom, missing a kidney.

"Three minutes in the microwave ought to do it," the

woman said. She had lipstick on her teeth and her hair was swept back in a curled tail. "I've brought two forks."

"That's very kind of you, but I've just eaten. I'm sure it's lovely, thank you."

"Let me buy you a drink, Ollie. We can chat for a bit."

"That'd be nice, but I have a lot more carriages to get through."

"Just a quick drink. We can make it a stiff one."

Oliver tried not to let his laugh sound dismissive. He glanced at Annabelle who had stepped away to give the casserole dish to one of the train attendants.

"I'm sure we can find something to talk about if we go somewhere private."

"It's a lovely offer, honestly, but as you can see, I've got a lot of other people to meet."

She was in her late forties, he guessed. Some women were convinced they could straighten him out. "You just haven't met the right woman yet," one lady said. She was the compere of a karaoke night in a backwater bar, and she sang three love songs to him while leaning across his table, pushing her breasts towards him with as much slutty seduction in her eyes as she could manage.

He humoured her for a while before realising that he was perpetuating her myth that maybe she could be the one to turn him. "I don't need to be fixed," he said in the end. "You're sweet, but I am who I am."

He had left the bar and never returned, but on *The Duchess of Dublin*, he had no option to walk away.

The woman stepped into his safe zone. "Call me Sally. I can give you a night you'd never forget."

"I would absolutely never forget it but, please, Sally, you do understand that I'm gay, don't you?"

"I don't mind if you don't. You can close your eyes. I'll make it special."

"Thank you, I'm going to walk away now."

He looked for Annabelle—she had no qualms with telling people to piss off.

Sally wrapped her arms around his neck and pulled him close with force. Her hand slipped down to his backside to cup his cheek. "Just hold me," she said, and at last the train representative stepped in to prise her away from him.

Annabelle was battling her way through the crowd.

"That's enough," the rep said.

Oliver stepped out of Sally's arms and leaned close to her. "Don't ever put your hands on me again."

When he looked at the bar, he watched Denis get off his stool with a scowl on his face. He walked back towards their private carriage and Oliver never felt more abandoned in his life.

13.

DENIS

enis watched Oliver as he worked the crowd. It was amazing to see; a celebrity who had been joking about the school nurse just a few minutes ago was being mobbed by a gaggle of girls. Denis didn't know how he'd react if anybody ever asked him for his autograph. He was mistaken once for an actor from *Fair City*, Ireland's longest-running soap opera, but he shut that down so fast that the girl's head must've been spinning.

"Oh my God," somebody nearby said as she came away from Oliver. "He's gorgeous."

Denis watched as Oliver crouched down to talk to a young girl and sign her T-shirt, and he wondered what it would be like to see your face printed everywhere you turned.

Oliver knew what he was doing. He smiled, winked and laughed with his adoring fans. He posed for selfies and allowed the girls to kiss his cheek.

Farther down the carriage, Denis locked eyes with the ticket inspector who had dragged him through the train before Oliver came to his rescue. It soured his mood, but he turned back to watch Oliver in the hope that his good looks would rekindle the heat in the pit of his stomach.

But when Oliver accepted a plate of food from one of the older women and looked far too comfortable in her arms as she whispered something to him, Denis' passion fell on its ass. He should have known Oliver was just like any other celebrity, waking up every morning with a different girl in his hotel room. Oliver Lloyd probably had a little black book filled with the names of his sexual conquests.

One of the train's representatives pulled the woman off him, but Oliver leaned in and whispered something to her before she was dragged away. Denis could imagine what he'd said.

When Oliver glanced in Denis' direction, Denis couldn't decipher the look on his face. He stood up, leaving his heart behind, and turned to go back to his cabin in Oliver's private carriage where he'd left his rucksack.

"He's so lovely," someone said as Denis passed her. He stopped himself from telling her otherwise.

As he approached the carriage door, a hand gripped his shoulder. He turned, expecting it to be the ticket inspector, but Tom's grinning face smiled down at him.

"Where the hell have you been, man? I've been looking everywhere for you. I thought you got caught and were kicked off the train."

Denis fist-bumped him when Tom held out his hand. "Shit. If you found me, it means my invisibility cloak has fallen off." He took a step back and inspected his fellow stowaway. There was more grease on his cheeks and forehead than there had been when they first jumped on board the train, and he was wearing a pair of navy overalls with the train's logo embroidered on the breast pocket in gold thread. "Should I ask?"

Tom picked some invisible lint from his overalls and grinned. "When I replaced that old lady's lightbulb, someone saw me coming out of her room and said the clock in their cabin was running slow. I guess it just spiralled from there."

"That doesn't explain the outfit."

"Probably best if you don't ask. Did you find that kid's mum?"

"Yeah. A lot has happened since then."

"You met Oliver Lloyd yet? Seems like a nice dude."

Denis looked over Tom's shoulder to find Oliver, and he saw the ticket inspector coming their way. "Yeah, he's all right, I guess. Celebrities, right? They're all the same. Look, I got to duck out. Inspector's getting close."

Tom made a derisory sound in the back of his throat and turned to the old man as he approached. "Hey, Mickey, I got you that pack of smokes you wanted, up by the staff room. Catch you there in ten?"

The ticket inspector's face cracked in a smile, and he slapped Tom on the back. "You're the best, Tommy-boy." He walked away, ignoring Denis.

"Like I said," Tom told him. "You just got to look like you belong."

"You're doing a better job of it than me. I'm going to head back to my cabin and lay low for a while."

As he left, Tom followed. "Six phone numbers I've got now. Women love a greasy mechanic. I'll let you pick one when we get off at Belfast. Would you like that? You want one of my girl's numbers?"

Denis popped the button to the next carriage. "Sounds fun, but…" He didn't know what else to say.

"But what?"

Denis stepped into the space between carriages and held his hand over the second button, reluctant to enter Oliver's private car with Tom in tow. "I guess what I mean is—I'm probably a bit gay."

"Probably a bit gay."

"Yeah."

Tom reached forward and pushed the door release button. As he did, Denis backed up. He had thought Tom was leaning in for a kiss. It struck him, in that micro-second, that a kiss from Tom was all he'd wanted a couple of hours ago. And now, he hoped it would never happen.

"Well," Tom said. "Do probably-a-bit-gay people still like a drink?" He pushed Denis into the carriage and the door swished closed behind them. Denis didn't have a chance to respond. "Woah. Classy. I've heard of quiet carriages on trains, but this takes the cake." He whistled his admiration and walked down the car towards the bar.

Denis said, "We should move on before Oliver Lloyd comes back."

"This is Lloyd's carriage? Nice one." He sat on a stool and nodded at the barman. "Jack and Coke, please."

Adam gave a questioning glance at Denis, but said, "One free drink for engineers, but that's your limit. And you should disappear before the carriage's ticket holder comes back. And what'll it be for you, Denis?"

Denis resigned himself to these new circumstances. "Beer, please. No, wait. I'll have a sparkling water, please."

"I'll have his beer along with my JD."

When Adam placed napkins on the bar and lined up their drinks, Tom said, "It's about time you admitted you were gay."

"You knew?"

"I knew since you were, like, twelve."

"So, Aaron knows, too?"

"Not unless you told him."

"Why didn't you let him know?"

"Not my place to say."

Denis turned his glass of sparkling water on its napkin like a dial. He looked at Tom's grease-stained fingers, at the nails embedded with black dirt, and he knew that Tom was attractive, but he no longer desired him. He didn't understand how you could be drawn to somebody for so many years, and then lose that interest in a second.

Yes, he did. Its name was Oliver Lloyd.

"I thought you would have freaked when you found out."

"Just because I'm from Clannon Village—population three-hundred Bible-bashers—doesn't mean I'm narrowminded. Does anyone else know?"

"After tonight? Probably everyone from Dublin to Cork."

"That explains it."

"Explains what?"

The carriage door opened, and Oliver came in. He backed away from the door as it closed and went to the bar. Adam was already opening another bottle of sparkling water.

"I need a scalding hot shower and a bottle of mouthwash."

"Oliver fucking Lloyd. How's it going, lad?"

Denis watched Oliver eyeing the supposed mechanic and then ignoring him. He took the glass Adam gave him and swilled the water around in his mouth before swallowing.

"Dude, I got to introduce you to my good friend Denis. You two would get along like a house on fire."

Oliver studied him. "Denis and I go way back."

"Way back," Denis agreed.

Tom sucker-punched Denis on the shoulder. "You didn't tell me you know Oliver Lloyd."

"It's just Oliver," Oliver Lloyd said. He sat on the

stool next to Denis.

Adam said, "It's probably time for engineers to go off and do some engineering."

"In a minute," Tom said. "Oliver, tell me—who's your agent? Give me their number. I sing a bit. Do you want to hear?"

Oliver's smile was pleasant, but Denis thought he saw undertones of derision in it. "If you sing at my agent, she'll likely bust your chops."

"He'd probably like that," Denis said.

"I'd definitely like that."

As Tom's face clouded in sexual imagery, Denis said to Oliver, "What happened to the walkthrough?"

"I got molested."

"Get in, son," Tom said.

"Molested?"

"This gross woman pretty much told me the names of our children and, worse, how she planned on conceiving them with me."

"That's disgusting," Tom said. "Am I right, Denny?" he leaned forward, reaching beyond Denis towards Oliver, and Denis wanted to stop his dirty hand from touching him. "Looks like she gave you a little present, too."

Denis glanced down as Tom pulled a skimpy pair of lace panties from Oliver's jacket pocket.

Oliver stepped off his stool and backed away from the offending item. "I'm going to burn this suit."

Tom stuffed the panties in the hip pocket of his

overalls.

The conversation was surreal. Denis wished Tom would leave, but also hoped he'd stay. At least with Tom there, he could get involved in a conversation with Oliver instead of muttering monosyllabic answers and stuttering through his infatuation.

"Why do women think they can just throw themselves at you and you'll fall into bed with them? Don't they know who I am?"

"They want to get you into bed *because* of who you are," Tom said.

"Well, it ain't happening."

"We should totally swap numbers. You can send the girls my way and in return, I can offer you—well, have you met my mate, Denis?"

Denis and Oliver exchanged a glance.

"Where's Annabelle?" Denis asked, to mask his confusion.

"She was running interference so I could escape." He stepped away from the bar and stared out the window.

"Dude," Tom whispered to Denis. "That's your queue."

"Huh?"

"You have got to be the dumbest smart person I know. Go and talk to him."

Tom turned back to Adam and asked for another Jack Daniels.

Denis wasn't sure what to do with his hands. He joined Oliver by the window and folded his arms.

"I'm sorry."

"What for?"

"I think I had you all wrong. I saw that woman throw herself at you and I made an assumption."

"You figured a rich twat like me would get his rocks off with anyone in a skirt."

"I never called you a twat."

"You didn't have to; it was written all over your face when we first met."

"I was a different person back then."

"Weren't we all?" Oliver said. "Who's your friend?"

"That's Tom. We got on the train together."

"So, you weren't lying when you said you were friends with one of the train engineers."

"Something like that."

"I'm sorry, too," Oliver said. Denis didn't ask why. He clamped his lips shut for fear of saying something awkward. Oliver took the hint. "I thought you were a bit of a twat, too."

"Maybe I am."

"Maybe you are. Maybe we all are."

A screech came from under the carriage and something in the walls sounded like it had rattled loose. Tom stood up. "Sounds like the brakes could be doing with some oil." He drained his glass, smacked his lips, and reached his dirty hand out to Oliver. "You're a legend, Oliver Lloyd. Drop into my Insta anytime." Oliver shook his hand and Tom pulled Denis into a hug. "You, me, and a bucket of Jack Daniels. Belfast isn't going to know what hit it."

When he was gone, the carriage was quiet. Even the engine seemed to stutter into silence for a moment.

"He seems like a good egg."

"He is. I didn't know how much of a good egg he was until tonight."

"Want to talk about it?"

Denis smiled and shook his head. "Not really."

They faced the window and stared out, but all Denis saw was their own reflection watching them. He stole a glance at Oliver's ghostly face and then looked away when Oliver's eyes met his.

He felt a warmth spreading over his cheeks.

"So," he said, with no idea what words would follow. "Old women who put their knickers in your pocket is not your thing?"

"The words 'old women' and 'knickers' really shouldn't be in the same sentence."

Denis nodded. The mood had shifted. They were talking, but they weren't doing so with the casual laughter they'd shared before Oliver's walkthrough. It felt deeper, even if their words were light.

He turned to face the real Oliver, not the reflection.

Oliver faced him, too.

And the train lurched. The squealing brakes groaned underneath them, and the lights flickered.

Denis tilted forward as Oliver faltered back on his heels. He reached out to catch Denis.

And Denis stumbled into his arms.

He stopped his fall by raising his hands, and as Oliver held him, his fingers found Oliver's strong chest.

They stood that way, for a second, in each other's arms.

"Sorry," Denis said, extracting himself from Oliver's limbs.

"Yeah," Oliver said. "No problem."

14.
OLIVER

enis' touch, the soft warmth of his hoodie against him when the train stuttered on the track, was like the memory of something he'd forgotten. Oliver wanted to feel it again. But Denis pulled away from him and Oliver turned to compose himself.

"I'm sure it's nothing," Adam said from behind the bar. He picked up the phone on the wall.

The train's brakes shrieked, and the carriage rocked with exertion. The lights flickered and dimmed, but as the train came to a stop, they brightened again, and the engine's soft hum vibrated beneath Oliver's feet.

Denis cupped his hands against the window to look at the night beyond. "There's nothing out there."

The engine coughed into silence.

Unsure what to do in the stillness that followed, Oliver joined Denis at the window. He could see nothing out there but the dark of an empty night.

"Feels like the start of a horror movie, right?" Denis said.

"If a killer clown comes through that door, I'm using you as a human shield."

"Sure. Sacrifice the little guy."

"I'll say something nice at your funeral. 'Here lies Denis Murphy. Eaten alive by a cannibalistic killer clown. Unrecognisable, but still good looking in a mangled way.'"

"Thanks," Denis said. "There won't be a dry eye in the house."

"If Mr Jangles gets his way, we'll all be dead."

"Who?"

Oliver narrowed his eyes and looked at him. "You don't know Mr Jangles the Clown?"

"Who?"

"Seriously? Only the most famous killer clown in movie history. 1967's *Mr Jangles Goes Berserk*. You've never seen it?"

"Is that in black and white?"

"Dude. We can watch it on Annabelle's iPad. Come on."

"Oliver," Adam said, "I think it's probably best if you stay put. I can't raise the engine room on the phone. They must be busy up there."

"Yeah," Denis said. "Annabelle will be back soon

enough, and you don't want to get mobbed again, do you?"

"I'm stuck on a train that's going nowhere." Oliver took Denis by the shoulders. "This is a matter of life and death. Killer clowns follow set rules and if you haven't seen *Mr Jangles Goes Berserk*, you don't know the rules."

He could see that Denis was trying to suppress a grin. "Well, why didn't you say so?"

"Come on. We have a clown to murder."

He entered the next carriage without looking back. He knew Denis would follow.

When Denis caught up with him, he said, "It's a good job you're not an actor. What was that all about?"

"I get antsy at these things when Annabelle disappears. Especially when there's some crazy loon onboard that may or may not try to do something stupid."

"I'm pretty sure Annabelle can look after herself."

"About eight months ago, some bloke threatened her with a knife. She says it was no big deal, but it freaked the hell out of me."

Oliver lowered his gaze as they marched through the carriage. In the stillness of a dead train, conversations had dropped to a whisper, and they hushed as he passed through them, like he was emitting a cone of silence. They started up again when he had moved on.

"Keep your head down and walk fast," Denis said. "I'm not your bodyguard."

"I wasn't lying about Mr Jangles. It really is the greatest killer clown movie ever made."

"If the train doesn't start moving soon, we'll have time to watch it." Denis pulled his phone out and raised it, searching for a signal. "We must be in the middle of Shitsville." The blue glow from his phone cast his face in an ethereal radiance and Oliver scanned the seated passengers to avoid staring at him.

"I think we passed Shitsville an hour ago. We're in Killer Creek now."

They moved into the next carriage without being accosted by passengers or killer clowns.

When she had disentangled herself from the casserole concubine, Annabelle was walking through the carriage towards them.

"There you are," Oliver said.

"We've had some crazies in our time, but that one is a juggler short of a circus."

Denis said, "We've got a clown she can borrow."

Oliver bumped knuckles with him when he offered his fist and they laughed.

"Have you two been sucking helium while I was gone?" Annabelle asked.

"Miss Blake?" a middle-aged man said.

Oliver looked over her shoulder as she turned to face him. He was slim and used an ornate cane to lean on. His hair was thinning but his face was kindly.

"Mr Lloyd isn't doing autographs right now," Annabelle told him.

"It's you I came to see, Miss Blake."

Oliver went to her side. "Miss Blake isn't doing

autographs right now, either."

The man ignored him. To Annabelle, he said, "Would you mind if we go somewhere a little bit more private?"

"We can talk openly here. Do I know you?"

When the man put his hand into the inner pocket of his jacket, Oliver gripped Annabelle's arm, conscious of having told Denis about the knife-wielding maniac a minute ago. He was grateful that Denis took up a position at Annabelle's other side.

"This is a photograph of me with my ex-wife and child." He held a Polaroid image towards her.

Annabelle refused to take it. "No."

"I just want to talk, Belle."

"I'm not doing this."

"Please. Just hear me out."

"Who let you on the train?"

"I bought a ticket, same as anyone else. When I heard Mr Lloyd was going to be here, I knew I had to see you."

"Now? After twenty years?"

Oliver stood between Annabelle and her father. "This is not the time or place, sir."

"I just want five minutes to explain."

He could feel the tension when Annabelle put her hand on his elbow and nudged him aside, and he saw how the passengers were staring at them. He was used to that, but Annabelle wasn't. "Do you want me to have him removed, Belle?"

She shook her head, eyed the man's walking cane, and set her jaw in defiance. "Where have you been?"

"London, mostly."

"Oliver, when were we last in London?"

"April. At the Marriott."

"We were in London in April," she told her father. "You didn't think to spring this on me there?"

Mr Blake cleared his throat and adjusted his grip on the cane. Whatever had befallen his hip or knee, Oliver could see that he was finding it difficult to remain standing.

"I'm not asking you to forgive me; just listen to my side. After that, I'll go."

"Belle?" Oliver asked.

"You don't have to," Denis said. Oliver admired him for speaking up under the circumstances, but he already knew how Annabelle would react.

"What happened to your leg?" she asked.

"Accident."

She nodded, turned, and straightened her back. "Follow me."

Oliver had watched her taking charge before. She could control a crowd, stave off the crazies, and hold a press conference all at once. But as she walked ahead of him, he could see that her energy was ebbing. The carriage was silent, save for the click of Mr Blake's walking cane on the wooden floor as he followed them.

When they entered Oliver's carriage, Annabelle went into one of the bedroom cabins and stood at the window, staring out with her hands pushed into the back pockets of her jeans.

Oliver held the carriage door from sliding closed as he waited for Mr Blake to catch up. "In there," he said, indicating the cabin. "And I don't need to tell you that if I hear raised voices, my friend and I will personally throw you off the train."

"I'm not here to cause harm, Mr Lloyd."

He stepped into the cabin and Annabelle said, "Leave the door open."

Denis filled his lungs and puffed up his cheeks in an awkward schoolboy manner. "Let's get a drink," Oliver told him.

At the bar, Denis said, "Two glasses of sparkling water and make them doubles."

"That bad?" Adam asked.

"Like you wouldn't believe," Oliver said.

He took his drink and swirled the ice in the glass. He knew Annabelle's father had disappeared twenty years ago, but she hadn't gone into much detail. She'd been seven, so she probably didn't know much.

"I'm assuming you've never met this guy?" Denis asked.

"He's been AWOL for twenty years, give or take. I've never even seen pictures of him."

"Is she going to be all right?"

He nodded. "I've never seen her look so broken. But yeah, she'll be okay."

He tried not to listen to the muffled voices further down the carriage. He couldn't understand the words, but he intuited the emotions they would convey—pain;

heartache; anger.

Twenty minutes later, Annabelle came out of the cabin, asked Adam for two cups of tea, and retreated again, closing the door behind her.

Denis had been pacing across the carriage with his phone in the air, trying to get a signal, and when he came back after Annabelle sequestered herself with her father, he said, "Must be going well. She wasn't covered in his blood."

Oliver could tell he meant it as a joke, something to lighten the mood, and although he didn't find it amusing, he was grateful that Denis was there. It was a distraction from the pain he'd seen in Annabelle's eyes before she returned to the cabin to continue her talks with her father.

"Have you got Plutonian Empire on that thing?" Oliver asked, pointing at Denis' phone.

"How old are you? No one has played Plutonian Empire in like ten years."

"I'm not good with phones."

"Do you even have one?"

"I do, but it's never switched on. Annabelle controls all that."

"What if you need to make a call?"

"I'm young enough to know nobody makes phone calls anymore."

"Fine, what if you need to send a text?"

"The only person I'd text is Belle, and she's usually at my side."

Denis sat on the stool beside him. "So, if I gave you my number, I shouldn't be expecting to ever hear from you?"

"For you, I might make an exception. But only to find out what you thought of *Mr Jangles Goes Berserk*."

"Fine," Denis said, exaggerating the word into two syllables like a spoilt teenager. "I'll watch your stupid dad movie. Jeez, get off my back already."

Oliver turned to Adam, who was putting two China cups on a tray for Annabelle. "I think I'm ready for this one to be thrown off the train now."

"Please. You'd miss me if I was gone."

"I can't tell if you're an angel sent to make me feel better or a devil sent to destroy my soul."

Denis shrugged his lips. "Maybe I'm both."

"I don't doubt it."

As Adam carried the tea tray to Annabelle's cabin, Denis said, "There hasn't been any shouting yet."

"I think that's worse than if there'd been a screaming match. When a woman goes quiet, that's when the trouble starts."

"What do you say to a man you haven't seen for twenty years?"

"Nothing that can fit into twenty minutes."

Adam came back with his lips clamped.

"They okay?"

"I don't know what's going on, but they're both alive if that's what you mean?"

"Doesn't look like we'll be carrying any dead bodies

off the train, then."

"Not fair," Denis said, and he walked back across the carriage with his phone in the air.

Oliver watched him. His sagging jeans revealed the white band of his Calvins where the hoodie had hitched up at the back and, for a second, Oliver couldn't look away.

The P.A. system crackled to life. "Ladies and gentlemen, Irish Rail apologises for the delay. We're experiencing some minor technical issues which should be resolved shortly. As soon as I have an update, I'll let you know. In the meantime, please sit back, relax and enjoy your evening." The announcement was repeated in Gaelic.

Oliver drummed his fingers on the bar. There had been nothing relaxing about this evening from the moment he got on the train.

The one saving grace was Denis.

15.
DENIS

Denis couldn't get a signal on his phone, and he knew it was pointless trying, but he inched along the carriage with his arm in the air because the alternative was to sit down beside Oliver and feel awkward.

Annabelle's inaudible conversation with her father continued in one of the cabins, and apart from the sound of Adam restocking the fridge with mini bottles of sparkling water, there was no other noise.

Trains stop on the tracks all the time; he knew that. He'd caught the train back from Dublin enough times late at night to remember the chill feeling of isolation in a quiet carriage while the driver waited for the signal to change. But this was different. Without the vibrating hum of the engine, the train felt abandoned, like a haunted carnival in the dead of night. It was like stepping on an escalator that wasn't moving, an uncomfortable jolt at the base of your solar plexus.

He had marched up and down the carriage twice with his phone held out before he gave up. When he yawned, he checked the time—after one—and asked Adam for a coffee. It was embarrassing, knowing he wasn't paying for any of this, but he promised himself he'd repay Oliver any expenses once he got home.

The thought of home made him wonder how Caroline was. She'd be asleep if Mum had calmed down enough by now to stop screaming. He wanted to hope that her overreaction to his coming out was nothing more than shock, but he wasn't sure of anything anymore. So much for unconditional love.

"I don't know how you can drink coffee this late," Oliver said.

"It stopped being late after midnight. Now it's early."

"You could go lie down; take a nap."

"I don't think I would sleep anyway. What about that movie you wanted me to watch?"

"The iPad's in with Belle and I don't have the balls to interrupt her."

Denis drank his coffee. He wanted to say Annabelle was lucky she could still talk to her dad, but that felt like opening up too much. Instead, he said, "If I had signal on my phone, we could order pizza."

"Yeah, sure. Just tell them to drop it by the side door of carriage G on the dead train in the middle of nowhere."

"I bet you've had some strange parcels from fans over the years."

"It's not like I'm in a boyband and getting tonnes of fan mail, but yeah, I've had some weird stuff delivered."

"Such as?"

"You're going to make me spell it out, aren't you?"

"Well, you've had a pair of knickers stuffed in your pocket tonight—could it get any worse than that?"

"At least those ones were clean."

Denis gagged and pushed his coffee away from him with distaste. Such an open display of revulsion to lady's underwear was, he hoped, enough of a clue for Oliver that women weren't his thing.

"How do you cope?" he asked.

"With dirty knickers? You throw them out and sterilise your hands."

"No, I mean with being famous. I'm lucky if the neighbours recognise me—you have the whole world staring at you."

"Oh, we're doing the deep-and-meaningfuls now, are we?"

"You have anything better to do?"

Oliver laughed. "I really don't." Denis saw how his body language changed. Oliver turned on his stool to face him more directly, but he also brought his arm across his chest towards the bar, refusing to expose his emotions. The juxtaposition of open earnestness with protective reticence was endearing. "Honestly, I don't think of myself as being famous. I mean, what am I famous for? I have a rich dad who owns most of Ireland's media resources and, because of him, I get to drive around in a custom-built Porsche Taycan, and I have someone to brush my hair every morning and tuck me in at night."

"Living your best dream," Denis said.

"You'd think, right? I don't know. The money's great; I've never wanted for anything—at least not material things. But being a celebrity is exhausting. Do you know the more money you have, the more free shit people give you? Only when you can afford the best do they send you free outfits in the hope you'll get snapped on Instagram wearing their clothes and shoes. And most of the time, celebrities only wear these things once and then they hang in a wardrobe for no one to get any benefit from. These shoes could probably feed a third-world village for a year. I should take them off."

"Don't take them off," Denis said. "So, being a celebrity isn't all rainbows and puppies?"

"If it was, you could sign me up twice; I love puppies. But the truth is, it's all yes-men and backstabbing. It's not unusual to find someone saying, 'Yes, sir; three bags full, sir,' while they actually stab your back."

"Annabelle's not like that."

"No. But she's not the first P.A. I've had. Not everyone is so conscientious." He paused before continuing. "Don't get me wrong. Most celebrities love the attention and the lifestyle that goes with it. We wouldn't have such a celebrity-obsessed culture if they didn't. But for me, it's a darkness that gnaws at the essence of my life. It chips away at me. So, to answer your question—how do I cope? I didn't. I spiralled. That's why I'm teetotal now. I went down a destructive path and got lost. It took me a while to claw my way back out."

"Shit, man," Denis said, touching Oliver's hand with compassion. His skin was soft and warm. "I didn't mean to bring up anything to upset you."

Oliver patted his hand, and his touch lingered. Denis couldn't meet his eyes and instead stared at their fingers. "I try to let the anger go. I have nothing against celebrities or the celebrity lifestyle. It just bugs me that people put me on a pedestal when I don't deserve it."

"You're a good guy. You deserve that recognition, at least."

Oliver pulled his hands away. "Celebrities don't get medals for being good guys."

"But they should."

Their eyes connected and Denis held his gaze. He'd been wrong about Oliver and the more time he spent with him, the more he could see he was not just an attractive man on the outside, but inside too.

When a knock hammered at the door that connected to the previous carriage, Adam stood up from behind the bar and said, "That's probably one of the engineers to explain what the hold-up is all about." He walked down the floor to answer it.

"Shouldn't the engineers be fixing whatever the problem is, not doing house calls?" Denis asked.

Adam pushed the unlock button that stopped anyone

unwanted coming through into the private carriage, and as the door opened, Oliver jumped off his stool.

"Oliver, darling," the woman called as she pushed her way inside. "We didn't get to enjoy our casserole, yet."

The crazy woman, whose knickers were currently in the pocket of Tom's overalls, slipped past Adam and tottered down the carriage in her heels. Her mascara had run, creating spiked lines of disaster around her cheeks, and her hair had come loose from whatever band or comb failed to contain it.

Oliver raised his hands as if to ward her off, and Denis stood beside him. He would never consider himself masculine enough to be a bodyguard, but under the circumstances, he would do his best.

"I saw you in Dublin last year; do you remember? I was wearing the pink lacy number. You were with that awful man. What was his name?"

"Walt," Oliver said. The word came quick to his lips, as though he spoke at her command.

Her words were slurred. "I want to kiss you, darling. Just a little kiss."

Adam came up behind her, but she brushed him off. His outstretched arms had been nothing more than a warning, a feigned block. Denis didn't blame him. No one wanted a lawsuit these days. "That's enough, young lady," Adam said, though she was older than him.

She shook her head and the heel of her shoe buckled underneath her. Adam saved her from falling.

"I think it's time you returned to your own carriage,

Sally," Oliver said. It struck Denis that he'd remembered the woman's name. "Maybe a little coffee is in order, don't you think?"

"I'd rather drink you." Her fingers reached for her breast as if to expose herself, but Oliver stepped forward with his arms wide—not for a hug, but to block her passage.

"Come on, Sally. This way, please."

"I've loved you for years, Ollie. I follow you on Facebook and Twitter and Instagram." Her face flushed as though she was about to either vomit or climax.

Oliver kept walking, his arms raised, forcing her backwards. Adam backed up behind her in case she stumbled.

"I'll have to give you my Trafick details, too. I tell you what, why don't we sit in your carriage where we can talk?"

"Let's go to your room where you can be a naughty boy, baby. I just love you so much."

"I know, Sally. Let's go outside."

She backed up and her heel buckled again. As she tripped, she reached out to grab Oliver. He stepped out of reach, and she went down hard on her knees.

Sally crawled towards him, incessant and insatiable. She was staring at his crotch.

"Please, now, Sally. Let's get you on your feet and back to your seat."

Denis had seen enough. He came forward and gripped her by the upper arm. He hefted her up and as she looked at him, he saw hatred in her face. "You've been asked to leave, lady."

"Get your filthy hands off me."

"Step back, Denis. It's okay."

"Come on. No one wants you here."

"Let me go before I rip your eyes out."

"I'll call security," Adam said.

"That's not necessary. Come on, Sally. Calm down."

Denis leaned closer to her, his hand still holding her arm. "Don't make me throw you off the train."

"Piss off, kid. I'm here for Ollie, not you." She tried to slap his face, but he ducked out of her way. Her sharp fingernails grazed his cheek but wouldn't leave any lasting damage.

"Jesus, woman."

"All right. That's enough." Annabelle stood behind them, in the open doorway of her cabin, her father watching over her shoulder.

"It's all right, Belle, we're handling it."

"The fuck you are." She strode towards them. "Denis, let go of her. You," she said, indicating Oliver, "go back to the bar. Adam, get the door." She stood toe to toe with Sally, who towered over her but wobbled in her drunkenness. "I'm not going to lay a hand on you. Not unless you make me. But you're going to get the fuck out of my carriage right now. D'you hear me?"

"I could knock you out, bitch."

"That's it." Annabelle pushed her and Sally staggered backwards. She didn't fall, but the momentum carried her towards the door. Annabelle kept pace with her. "Keep going. If I see your face again, I'm going to throw you under the train and personally drive this thing over the top of you." She pushed her again. "Get out."

As Sally passed into the gap between carriages, Annabelle hit the button to close the door and then locked it. They could see Sally in the empty darkness, cursing at them through the glass.

Annabelle closed the curtain over the window.

She turned to them. "If anyone opens that door again, I'm going to shove you out there with her and be done with it." She went back into the cabin with her father and closed the door.

Denis looked at Oliver. "Was that some crazy Krav Maga shit, or what?"

Oliver flatted his lips, but Denis could see the laughter hiding behind them.

"I think we handled that quite well, don't you?"

"You realise she's going to sue the hell out of the pair of us, right?"

Denis said, "Not me. She doesn't have a clue who I am."

"I'll give her your name and address on my way off the train."

"You're such a pal."

"Always here to help." He raised his hand for a high five and Denis slapped it. Then Oliver pulled him into a hug.

It was a bro-hug, Denis told himself. Just two friends

squeezing out their bromance.

But it lasted for four Mississippis.

And bro-hugs don't last that long.

16.

OLIVER

Oliver slapped Denis' back when he realised their hug was going on too long, and he pulled away. Denis cleared his throat as he retreated to the window with his phone in the air, like he hadn't already walked up and down the carriage a million times, searching for a signal.

He could still hear the muffled annoyance of Sally in the connecting carriage as she gave her tirade against the curtained window, and he was thankful for Annabelle's intervention. She was right—he wasn't handling it. Sally scared him. Confrontation wasn't his strong suit, not since he quit drinking. A year ago, if he'd been as drunk as she was, maybe he'd have screamed in her face, prodded at her nerves until she lashed out at him. Now, he tried to be as accommodating as possible, even when he was trying to get rid of her. You don't talk to drunk people the same way you talk to sober ones.

He heard a groaning sigh from Denis and when he looked up, he saw him slumped in one of the bucket seats by the window.

"This is ridiculous. How did people entertain themselves on long-distance journeys before the invention of phones?"

"I spy with my little eye," Denis said, "something beginning with boredom."

"That's not how you play."

"Fine, then come and stare out the window with me and play Red Car, Blue Car. Every time I see a red car, I get to punch you in the arm."

"You know what this carriage needs? A piano."

"Do you play?" Denis asked.

"No. Do you?"

"I never had the fingers for it."

Adam replaced their drinks without being asked, and he said, "I've got some board games behind the bar if that'll help?"

Denis rubbed his hands with glee. "As long as it's not Monopoly. I turn into a monster-overlord-dictator with Monopoly."

Oliver smiled at Adam who stooped down behind the bar to pull out the games. He'd played the junior version of Trivial Pursuit with his niece, Shiva, a few months ago, but apart from that, he'd never really had time for board games before, not even when he was young.

"Nice one," Denis said when Adam sat a stack of game boxes on the bar. "Let's play chess."

"That's the one with the popes and the horses, right?"

"Bishops and knights. Don't you know how to play, posh-boy?"

"How come you do, gutter-boy?"

"Touché. My dad taught me. Come on, it's easy."

Oliver eyed the stack of boxes and shook his head. "Teach me some other time. Here's the perfect game." He pulled out one of the boxes and held it up for Denis and Adam to see.

"No way."

"Yes way."

He had selected Twister and, even as he lifted the lid off the box, he regretted it. He wasn't sure if he could trust himself in such close bodily contact with Denis.

"Twister's for little kids."

"So? Be a kid for once."

He unfolded the plastic matt of colourful circles and spread it on the floor of the carriage. It fit snuggly between the wall of the bar and the windows on the far side. He took his suit jacket off and kicked his brogues into the corner.

Before he could tell Denis to take his trainers off, the sound of shattering glass interrupted him.

Annabelle and her father came out of their cabin. "What the hell was that?" she asked.

Oliver opened the cabin door opposite Annabelle's, and he saw a fist-sized rock on the carpeted floor. The room was covered in broken glass and a cool breeze swept across them.

Denis came up behind him and nudged him aside. "Stand back, you have no shoes on." He crunched over the glass in his trainers and looked out the window.

Oliver heard someone yelling. "See anything?"

"Bunch of kids. Someone's chasing them. Wait—it's Tom."

Even from the doorway, Oliver heard Denis' engineer friend shouting, "If I catch you, you little toerags, I'll tear your heads off for damaging my train."

Oliver picked his way over the glass to stand next to Denis. He saw a kids' play area at the far end of a field, and half a dozen lads running away. They couldn't be any older than twelve. Tom, his long legs pounding the grass, was giving chase, but they were too far for him to catch up to them.

At the edge of the playground, he stopped, caught his breath, and turned back to the train with a shake of his fist. When he stood by the carriage, below the broken window, he said, "I'll see if I can get something to board this up. You guys all right?"

"It's a bedroom. No one was in the room when it happened."

"Just close the cabin door. We'll be on the move soon enough."

Denis said, "Tom, what are you doing out there?"

Tom slapped the wall of the train. "Being one of the good guys for a change."

Looking out of the window, Oliver could see the steam engine at the head as the track curved. There was no smoke coming from the chimney.

He closed the cabin door behind him as they came out, and he removed his socks to make sure there was no glass stuck to them.

Adam produced a key and locked the door.

"Well," Annabelle's father said. "That's enough excitement for one day."

"You're telling me," Annabelle said.

Oliver gave her a questioning look and her subtle nod said she'd tell him everything later.

Mr Blake stood with an awkwardness that Oliver could tell was not just from his limp. His knuckles were white where he gripped his cane.

Annabelle offered him her hand and he shook it. She punched the door release button at the end of the carriage without a word, and when it sliced open, Mr Blake nodded at her, smiled, and left.

"I could do with a tequila," Oliver said, and he meant it. The temptation was always there, though he tried hard to push it away.

"Do you guys want a minute?" Denis asked as he backed up towards the bar.

Annabelle smiled and shook her head. "Not right now. I need to be alone."

"Denis, I'll be back in a few minutes."

Annabelle raised her hand to stop him. "Just let me have a minute, Ollie. I'm fine. We'll talk later." She went back into her cabin and closed the door.

"I should go with her."

He felt Denis' hand on his forearm. "You heard her. She probably just needs a minute to regroup her thoughts. She'll come out when she's ready."

They went back to the bar.

"What kind of parent lets their teenage brats run rampant at two A.M.?" Adam asked.

"The kind that never played Twister with them when they were younger," Denis said.

"Oh, we're doing this now?"

Denis kicked his high-tops off and made a display of stretching out his limbs as though he was about to run a three-minute mile. Before handing the spinner to Adam to oversee the game, Oliver glanced at Annabelle's room. He couldn't read her face before she locked herself away, and Mr Blake's expression had been one of pain from leaning against his walking cane for prolonged periods. He'd never seen Belle so closed off from him and, as much as he wanted to know what her father had to say for himself, he dreaded bringing the subject up when he saw her next.

"Who goes first?" Adam asked, spinning the dial.

"Age before beauty?" Oliver suggested.

"Old age before younger beauty," Denis said.

"I'm almost certain that was a thinly veiled insult."

"I don't know what you're talking about."

"Left foot green," Adam said.

By the third round, Oliver had both feet on the

colourful circles, and his right hand in the middle of the matt. Denis had entered the game with his right foot and moved it twice based on Adam's spins. He was still upright and had only one foot on the board.

"Left hand blue," Adam instructed Denis. He crouched and put his hand on the indicated circle. So far, their bodies weren't twisted together as the game would suggest, and Oliver was disappointed. He realised it would have been far more intimate with more than two players, but there was no one else he wanted to get close to.

He upped the stakes. When Adam said, "Right foot red," Oliver extended his leg towards Denis and eased it into place.

"If your feet stink, I'm calling foul play," Denis said, turning his face away from Oliver's outstretched toes. "That's an unfair advantage."

"All's fair in love and Twister."

"Left foot yellow," Adam said.

The grin on Denis' face told Oliver exactly where it was going to slide. Denis pushed out and eased his toes onto the furthest yellow spot he could reach, directly under Oliver's face.

His leg had slipped between Oliver's and now the game was mimicking its name. His sock overhung his toes like it no longer wanted to be attached to him.

Oliver made a display of retching as the foot slid under him, but there was no foul smell. He could see the fine hairs above Denis' ankle where the leg of his jeans had ridden up and Oliver wanted to lean down and press his lips against the pale flesh.

"Ready?" Adam asked. "Oliver—right hand red."

He assessed the battlefield. There was an easy target within reach, but there was much more fun in being tactical. He reached under himself, past Denis' thigh, and dropped his hand on a red circle.

Denis struggled to stay aloft. He wobbled and, with the cry of a slain warrior, he collapsed on Oliver's arm. They tumbled together, an awkward mess of limbs and laughter. Oliver slapped Denis' leg until he shifted his butt enough to let him remove his arm. He twisted so that he lay on his back, shoulder to shoulder with Denis.

Their laughter rippled over the bar as Adam shook his head and walked away.

"I can't tell who won," Oliver said, his cheeks hurting.

"I didn't fall, I was pushed."

"Like Humpty Dumpty?"

Denis stopped laughing and turned to him in confusion. "What?"

"Like Humpty Dumpty. He didn't have a great fall, he was pushed."

"Dude."

"Dude."

Their laughter rose to fill an otherwise quiet carriage. In time, it became a subtle cough, and soon they lay in silence, on the plastic game mat, their chests rising in unison. Oliver felt the heat from Denis' body, and he remembered the hug they'd shared. It stirred thoughts of longing in the pit of his stomach, of naked sex on the carriage floor.

"Why did you stop drinking?"

Denis' question cut short any visions of sex. Oliver cleared his throat.

"You don't have to answer that. Sorry."

"It's okay."

"No, seriously. I shouldn't have asked."

Oliver stared at the ceiling. He could imagine the only other time he'd ever lie on the floor of a train is if drink really was involved. When he didn't answer at once, Denis turned as though to stand, but Oliver reached out and pulled him back to the mat. He said, "When you wake up at ten A.M. with a brain-splitting hangover from the night before—a night you can't even remember because you drank so much—and you decide the only way to cure that hangover is to crack open a fresh bottle of tequila, you can do one of two things. You either drink yourself drunk again, or you get up and you do something about it."

"Just like that? You just decided to stop?"

"No. I sank lower first. You see, most people drink to enjoy themselves, to have fun. It loosens you up, right? Me, I drank to get lit. I needed to be wasted. For you, it's a buzz. You can talk to that fit person across the bar. And maybe you go back to theirs and you have sex, and the sex is probably good. But for me, I'll never know how good it was because when I woke up in the morning, I wouldn't even remember chatting that person up, let alone going back to theirs. I'd end up rifling through their mail for an address just so I can call a taxi to get the hell out of there before they woke up. There are entire weeks of my life that I don't remember. One time, I went out for drinks in Dublin on a Thursday night and the next thing I remember is waking up in a hotel in Budapest. On the following Monday."

"Sounds like a laugh."

"I thought so at the time. But seriously, it's horrible having these holes in your memory. And getting home wasn't easy. Do you know how difficult it is to find an Irish embassy in Hungary?" He collected his thoughts before continuing. "I'm not one of those guys that say drink is evil, but it definitely made me do the devil's work."

"You sound like my mum."

Oliver twisted so that he faced Denis. Denis' smile was soft and warm.

"I'll take that as the compliment you didn't intend it to be."

He watched Denis blink twice before he spoke. "So, you checked yourself into rehab?"

"After I broke up with my ex, yeah. Walter was one of those guys that get under your skin. He certainly got under mine. He was no good for me and, in truth, I was probably no good for him. I checked out of the relationship and into rehab." He smiled at the memories of his time at The Darlington Manor, even though it had been a difficult two weeks. "The first three nights, I screamed until I was hoarse. And this burly Jesuit priest who was easily seven feet tall and built like a tank—he held me in his arms and rocked me until I stopped screaming and the tears dried up and he gave me a tissue to wipe the snot from my face.

"Father Bartosz—he was Polish—sat in an armchair in my room, reading aloud from his bible in a language I found incomprehensible. But it wasn't the words that soothed me, it was his voice, this gruff, smoker's wisdom that filled my lungs with peace. And in the mornings, when I woke with a head full of cotton wool and a mouth full of bile, he would still be there, asleep in the armchair just as he had been the night before. That priest saved my life. I'm not religious, not in the slightest, but if I was, Father Bartosz would be my god."

"Do you miss it?"

"Rehab? Or alcohol?"

"Both, I guess."

Oliver closed his eyes. "Every damn day."

When he opened them again, Denis' face was no more than six inches from him, and his eyes were cloudy in the dim light from above. Oliver saw the sheen of moisture on his lips. "I don't want you to think that you can't have a drink around me," he said. "I face my demons—every day. But I'm stronger than they are. I have to be. If you want a drink, I won't be offended."

Before Denis could respond, the lights in the carriage flickered and dimmed. Oliver hadn't noticed the electrical hum they produced but as the bulbs died and an absolute silence took over, he felt a stillness that he hadn't experienced since his final nights at The Darlington Manor.

In the darkness, Denis said, "I never want to offend you."

"You can't." Oliver felt Denis' breath in front of him. He wanted to lean forward, to cup his face in his hands and kiss him. But his body refused to move.

And then the emergency backup lights illuminated them.

They were still staring at each other when Annabelle came from her room and said, "What're you doing on the floor?"

Oliver said, "Looking for Jesus."

17.
DENIS

Denis was moved by Oliver's words. Deciding on the need for intervention in his drinking was brave and empowering. But, more than that, the overriding thought in Denis' mind was not of Oliver's strength of character, but the smell of his cologne and the closeness of his body as they lay together on the colourful plastic mat.

It was obvious now like it should have been hours ago—Oliver was into him. There was no doubt in his mind. He was certain in the darkness before the murky backup lights came on that Oliver wanted to reach out and kiss him. It wasn't just wishful thinking.

There had been a moment when he thought he, too, was going to lean forward, but fear stamped its claw on his neck and pinned him down. When Annabelle came out of her room and they got off the floor, she and Oliver spoke in hushed confidence away from the bar, and Denis stood by the window and analysed that fear.

He was not afraid of men. Or sex. He had been intimate before and knew what he was doing. The fear came not from inexperience with a man, but from the potential for rejection. This was not about sex but about feelings. He feared rejection of his soul, not his body.

Oliver wasn't the celebrity socialite he first assumed. There was a depth to him that Denis wanted to explore. He needed to climb the mountain that was Oliver Lloyd. Although he wanted to get into bed with him and touch him in places he could only dream of, his thoughts also ran to curling up on the couch together, reading books as a thunderstorm shocked the world outside, rain battering the window, and an open fire making shadows gyrate around them.

He was a solitary man, but he wanted to share his solitude with somebody else.

He sensed that Oliver wanted something more than friendship from him, but he couldn't tell if he wanted to share the brightness of his afternoons or just the darkness of his nights.

He glanced at Oliver as he spoke with Annabelle. It must have been a blow for her, seeing her father for the first time in years. He didn't know what bad blood had flown down the river between them in the past, and he tried to imagine what kind of heartache would create their estrangement. If he had the opportunity to see his own dad again, he would jump at the chance. But if his mum refused to see him as her son, despite his sexuality, maybe they'd suffer the same fate.

He imagined bumping into her thirty years from now at a supermarket. Her age-blemished face would look at him, at first without recognition, then understanding would creep across her eyes. And maybe she'd avert her gaze, but it was too late, they'd seen each other. And Denis would be the first to speak. He wouldn't say *Hello, Mum*. He'd just say, "Hello."

And she'd nod her acknowledgement of him as though he was some old neighbour who had moved away years before and was almost forgotten, lost in a memory box of other neighbours who had come and gone.

"This is Oliver," he'd say, indicating the tall man who stood beside him, handsome in his khakis and comfortable loafers. Oliver would extend his hand and she'd take it gingerly, and her smile would be cursory and short.

They'd exchange a few words about the weather and how well Caroline is doing in her new job in finance over in London. And then she'd make her excuses—parked on double-yellow lines; left the oven on; forgot to feed the budgie—and Denis would check his watch and say they had a function to attend, something they couldn't get out of, terribly sorry.

"See you around," he'd say. And they'd walk away. He probably wouldn't shop at that supermarket again. And their estrangement would carry on as though that blip had never been.

"You okay?" Oliver asked.

Denis nodded. For a moment, he was too angry at his mother to speak. He cleared his throat. "Is she?" Annabelle had assumed her position at the bar and Adam was fixing a drink for her—an alcoholic cocktail that he was shaking the life out of.

"She will be. Her dad apologised for a lot, but she's not ready to forgive him yet."

"I wasn't trying to pry."

"I know."

"But she will be okay, right?"

"It's nice to see that you care."

"If she's the P.A. to the great Oliver Lloyd, of course I care."

"You make me sound like a magician. The Great Oliver Lloyd and his sidekick, Marvellous Mefisto."

"Yeah, but can you make a train disappear?"

Oliver reached out and covered Denis' eyes with the palms of his hands. "Alakazam."

"You astound me."

"That's what I want." He turned to the bar and asked Adam if there was any update on the status of the train.

"Nothing yet."

"Whatever the problem is, it doesn't bode well for its maiden voyage," Annabelle said. Her face was serene as she sipped from her martini glass.

"I'm sure they'll get it up and running again in no time."

Denis said, "If they don't get the power back on soon, we'll freeze to death. Or starve."

"I won't," Annabelle said. "Donner. Party of one. You'll be first on the menu when the food runs out."

"Ha ha."

"You laugh," Oliver said, "but she means it."

While Denis had been contemplating his fears and Oliver was speaking to Annabelle, Adam had packed away the game. Denis returned to the window and looked for the spotlights over the kids' playground that Tom had chased the youngsters through. In the dark of a clear night, it was an oasis among the brambles.

"Well, there's only one thing for it, then."

Oliver and Annabelle looked at him, their expressions one of mutual inquiry.

"We need to get out there and have a go on the swings."

"No way."

"Don't be a spoilsport."

Annabelle came to the window. "Well, that's not the creepiest thing I've seen all day."

"Are you scared?"

"No. But one of us needs to be a grownup. You guys go. I'll keep the train warm."

"I'm not going out there," Oliver said. "The train will take off without us and we'll be stranded."

"You're Oliver Lloyd," Denis reminded him. "The train won't leave without you."

"Go on," Adam said. "I have an emergency key for

the door. I won't tell anyone if you don't."

Oliver put his shoes on. As Adam unlocked the door and heaved it open, Oliver said, "If they start the engine, give us a holler."

Without a platform, there was a five-foot drop from the floor of the carriage to the rocky ground below. Denis sat on the edge, legs dangling, and jumped. When he turned back to the train, he held out his arms. "Do you need a hand, old man?"

Oliver dropped lightly to the ground beside him. "Save your old-man jokes for when I'm actually old."

"I've already ordered a tartan blanket for your knees."

A thin frost had formed on the long grass and, free from the stuffy carriage, Denis breathed in and exhaled, his breath clouding in front of his face in the chill air. They picked their way through the brown grasses and reeds that reached their waist and when they got to the edge of the playground, their clothes were wet with evening dew. This far from any light pollution, the stars were uncountable, and the only visible clouds were massing in a grey haze on the horizon. It was hard to imagine that it was only three days until Christmas.

Oliver laughed as he approached the turnstile roundabout in the centre of the playground. "Hop on, my lord, your carriage awaits." He waited until Denis stood between the support rails, said, "Hold on tight," and spun the roundabout.

As the world revolved, Denis leaned back against the central pillar, raised his arms, and tilted his face to the stars. In that moment, he was the centre of the universe and Oliver was his guide, turning the sky so that the stars kaleidoscoped around him.

When Oliver stopped the ride, Denis was dizzy, but he was laughing.

Oliver climbed the steps of the slide and on his way down he got stuck. His suit trousers had caused too much friction on the metal base and Denis couldn't catch his breath from laughing too much.

Oliver shunted his way to the bottom with a grumble.

For a few minutes, Denis pushed Oliver on a swing, following through with his arms for maximum momentum, but in time he took a seat on the second swing and, without declaring their intentions, they competed to see who could swing the highest.

When Oliver skidded his heels in the dirt, Denis had one more swing before braking. "I won."

"You did not win. I got two feet higher than you."

"Not a chance." When Oliver didn't rebuff his accusation, Denis turned to him, keeping his hands on the metal chains of the swing. Oliver's face had lost its laughter.

"Can I ask you a question?"

Here it was, Denis thought. The end of their fun. He didn't speak.

"Are you ready to tell me why you snuck on the train now?"

"Wait, didn't I tell you already?" Denis asked, trying to make light of the situation.

"Denis."

"Okay."

"Well?"

Denis rocked on the swing but not so much that his feet left the ground. He was right: this was the end of their fun. The words that left his mouth now would forever redefine whatever friendship he had developed with Oliver Lloyd.

He considered lying. Instead, he said, "I came out to my mother tonight." He stopped rocking the swing and he let his leg jiggle like he was trying to burrow his toes in the ground. He looked ahead of him at the train rather than face Oliver. It was a black silhouette in front of a dark blue sky, crowned with stars.

"She didn't take it well. She kicked me out. It's not like she's religious or anything, not normally, but tonight she disowned me because God hates fags, apparently. Caroline, my little sister—you'd like her, she's ballsy—she tried to stick up for me, but my mum's not the kind of person you go against, not if you want to survive. Especially not if you're living under her roof. I'm lucky, I got out. I went to college in Dublin. But Car, she's just sixteen. She's still at home. Sticking up for me is going to make her life a misery. I can't wait until she finishes school and comes to Dublin. Or anywhere. Away from her. Away from hell.

"Anyway. I told Mum I was gay, and she threw me out of the house. I had time to pack a few things, and then I headed across town to the bridge where—well. I stopped on this bridge, and I wondered what the hell my life was all about. What is anyone's life about? Why the fuck are we here? And Tom—you know Tom."

"The engineer."

"Yeah. Except he's not a train engineer. He's a car mechanic. Anyway. He saw me on the bridge and told me about this train he was going to sneak onto and did I want to come. And I had nothing better to do." He looked at Oliver. "So that's why I snuck on your train."

Oliver looked pensive. Before he spoke, he leaned back on the swing as if he was about to move it, but he didn't. He said, "Your mum probably just needs some time."

"Yeah."

"She'll get over it. It was just a shock."

"Yeah."

"She'd have been expecting grandkids and stuff. Just give her a minute to process it."

"Yeah."

The silence that fell between them was a wedge that stove the fabric of reality. Here they were, in a kids' playground, sitting on a pair of swings and talking about his sexuality. If the multiverse theory was correct, in some other universe they were already sleeping together.

And in another, they had never met.

Oliver twisted his swing so that he faced him. He said, "The world keeps spinning no matter who's on it. You know what that says to me? It says God doesn't care who's gay or straight or bi or trans. If God had an issue

169

with that, he'd stop the world from turning. But it keeps on spinning, and we keep on breathing. Life's not about procreating. It's about living. It's about being who you are. And if who you are is not what your mother wants you to be, who cares? God doesn't. The universe doesn't. You've got to be your true self and learn to live with it. Life and death—we all suffer them. It doesn't matter what your sexuality is, none of us gets out alive."

Denis sighed and felt the hurt leaving his body.

He turned to face Oliver.

And Oliver looked at him. "Feel better?"

"Yeah."

"Good."

Denis tried to smile but knew that his lips weren't working.

And Oliver leaned in.

Denis closed his eyes.

He felt Oliver's breath on his face before their lips met.

And although nothing other than their lips touched, Denis felt the entire universe expand around him.

Kisses were like that. With the right person, they made your brain explode.

18.

OLIVER

"Wow," Oliver said. He didn't mean to; it just came out.

He flattened his lips and could taste Denis on them. Love never crept up on him. It hit him in the face with the full force of a steamroller. It had been his downfall in the past. Walter was a prime example.

He closed his eyes when Denis came in for a second kiss. He was aware of every atom of his body fighting for the closeness of Denis' touch. Oliver parted his knees and allowed Denis to slip between them, the movement fluid as they were suspended from the swings. His pulse quickened and beat a powerful rhythm in his chest.

When their lips parted, Denis didn't pull away. He lowered his forehead into the crook of Oliver's neck and nuzzled there. Oliver stroked his arm.

"Wow," he said again.

Denis laughed against his skin. It was a nervous laugh, Oliver knew, quiet and unsure.

He could feel himself becoming aroused, but he didn't want to spoil the moment. He pushed back his thoughts and ran his hand over Denis' shoulder.

Denis nodded against him as though he'd been asked a question, and when he looked up, Oliver saw a shine in his eyes that hadn't been there before.

"I'm going to kiss you again," Denis said.

"Yeah?"

"If that's okay."

"Do I have any time to think about my answer?"

"No."

"Okay, then." And he couldn't help but smile as Denis came towards him, ruining—or making perfect—an otherwise simple manoeuvre. They laughed. And then they kissed.

Oliver cupped his face as he had wanted to on the floor of the train—wanted to and never thought possible.

The chains of the swing creaked and clanked above him.

When they parted this time, Denis pulled away and their swings returned to their natural places beside each other. Oliver felt an emptiness at once.

Denis didn't look at him, locking his gaze on the distant train.

"That was…" Oliver said, but he had no words to

finish the sentence.

"It was."

Oliver wanted to tell him he was a good kisser, but he realised the thought would make him sound like a lovestruck twelve-year-old. He wanted to taste those lips again, to ease his tongue between them and feel the pressure of Denis against him. Instead, so as not to completely lose the physical connection, he reached out and took Denis' hand. His skin was soft and cold.

"Merry Christmas," Denis said, but it sounded like he was saying it to himself. His fingers closed tighter around Oliver's.

It was the worst possible time to speak, but Oliver needed Denis to hear him. "Your mum will get over it. I promise."

"You don't know her."

"She can see how amazing you are, I'm sure."

"You're just saying that because you kissed me."

"No. You kissed me, remember?"

"That's not my recollection of events, your honour."

"To be honest, my brain went to mush for a minute. I can't remember who started it. I'm just glad it happened."

"The absolute best moment of your life, right?" Denis smiled.

"I know what you're doing."

"What?"

"Knocking yourself down by making a joke of it. What if it was the best moment of my life?"

"I'd be asking for my money back."

"You're doing it again. Take a damn compliment."

"Okay," Denis said, but Oliver knew he didn't mean it.

Oliver let Denis' hand slip away when his fingers relaxed, and he watched as he pushed back on the swing and released. He gave him a moment of silence before getting off his own swing and holding his hand out. "Come on. Let's race."

"Race? In those shiny shoes? You know I'd win."

"Not on foot," Oliver said, pointing across the playground to a pair of wooden horses on springs. "On those."

The springs, embedded in the ground, allowed children to rock back and forward but little else. They were tiny when they approached, but Oliver straddled one, gripped the handlebars that doubled as ears, and sat down. "Starting positions, please." When Denis took the other horse, Oliver said, "And they're off." He rocked the horse like a lunatic.

Denis whooped and spoke like a commentator. "Mr Rainbow Sparkles coming up the inside. Will he take the Championship for the third year in a row? Miss Trixie Lott had a massive lead, but the gap is closing." Oliver reached across and tried to push him off the horse, but Denis kept riding. "Manhandling a fellow jockey— that'll cost him. And Mr Rainbow Sparkles powers into pole position. It's neck and neck. It's too close to call. It's a photo finish. And Mr Rainbow Sparkles has done it. The podium is his. Miss Trixie Lott can only weep in disgust."

Oliver fell off the horse, dizzy with laughter.

When Denis stood over him, he held a hand up—not to be lifted from the ground but to beckon Denis down. They lay beside each other on the wet ground, staring up at the stars.

When his breathing had returned to normal, Oliver said, "Do you ever wonder how many other planets out there are like ours?"

"There can't be any other planet out there that makes half of their people feel as bad as we make ours."

"I bet there's a planet populated solely by puppies. No one can ever feel bad around puppies. And they don't ever grow up; they just stay puppies forever. Ninety-year-old puppies. That's what we need."

"And maybe," Denis said, "there's a planet that only has gay men."

"How would they reproduce?"

"It happens when their nipples touch another man's nipples—which would be wholly inappropriate to do in a supermarket. And by law, the man who initiated the nipple-kiss would be the one to carry the child. And he'd have to carry it for eighteen years and when it was born, passed like a gallstone, it'd be a fully-grown adult ready to venture out into the world and earn a living. No one gets to sponge off their parents in that world."

Oliver shifted onto his side. "Okay. So, by that logic, what if I was walking down the street and not paying attention to where I was going. And I came around a corner and bumped into another man. And our nipples had nipple sex. What happens then?"

"If you're clothed, your nipple spunk wouldn't penetrate the other man."

Oliver retched. "Nipple spunk. I have never been more turned off in my life."

"You don't want my nipple spunk?"

"Can we please stop saying nipple spunk?"

"I don't think I can."

"I hate you."

"No, you don't."

"No. But I want to."

"There's also probably a world out there filled with lesbians," Denis said.

"Stop. I don't want to know how they reproduce."

"Good. Because I really know nothing about the female body."

"When I was a kid," Oliver said, realising how silly the memory was even as he said it, "my mum refused to let my dad get a Volvo because it sounds too much like vulva."

"That's a lady part, right?"

Oliver motioned with his hand. "Somewhere down in the lady garden, I believe."

"You can learn to hate a man very quickly, you know."

"Right?"

Oliver leaned back and looked at the stars. The mention of his mother soured his mood, and he wondered if Denis felt the same. His own mum didn't bat an eyelid when he came out. He couldn't imagine her having an opinion about his love life, in either direction, the way Denis' mum had. People use religion to hide behind their fears. Denis had said she wasn't usually religious, but he knew better. Most Irish people were devout when it suited them. He was convinced Denis' mother would get over her initial anxieties and learn to deal with it, but he didn't want to say those words aloud and upset Denis again.

Here, in the darkness of a clear winter night, lying on the rubber tiles of a children's playground at two A.M., Oliver wanted the night to pause. He wanted the sand-timer of life to be knocked on its side so that for now—for eternity—he could lie here with Denis and never move.

He put his hand on Denis' chest and felt the muscles tighten. They kissed again, their bodies pressed together, their souls entwined, and when they stopped, Oliver sighed. Denis' breath was like fruit salad.

Denis said, "How do you live your life in the public eye?"

"I don't. I mean, I became an alcoholic, didn't I?"

"But you're not anymore."

"I am. I just don't drink anymore." He closed his eyes and pressed his forehead against Denis'. "Honestly, being a Lloyd isn't easy and it isn't fun. If this—us—is going to last longer than between here and Belfast, you need to know what you're getting into." When Denis didn't respond, Oliver said, "I don't want to jump the gun. Sorry."

Denis snorted. "I jumped that gun with our first kiss on the swings. I don't want a one-night stand."

"Good. I don't, either."

"But I don't know about this whole celebrity thing."

"I'm not a celebrity."

"Yes, you are."

"No. I'm famous because my dad is a celebrity. I'm just a by-product of his fame. I'm a nobody, really."

"You're not a nobody."

"To society? Or to you?"

"Both?"

Oliver sighed and nodded. He turned onto his back again and laced his fingers with Denis'. To the sky, he said, "I wish I could just walk away from it all, head into the countryside and buy a house in the middle of nowhere, miles from everything. I'm sick of being Oliver Lloyd. I just want to be Jimmy Jones, Nobody Extraordinaire."

"But I like Oliver Lloyd."

"You just met me."

"And now I'm lying on the ground with you between the horses and the seesaw, holding hands and wanting to kiss you all over. Jimmy Jones wouldn't make me feel that way."

"You don't know Jimmy Jones very well. He'd have you writhing in ecstasy before you knew it."

"I'd like to see him try."

"That can be arranged." He closed his eyes, but when all he could see was a naked version of Denis, he opened them again. "Seriously, though. I want to run away, buy a house somewhere, and live off the land. Someplace near the sea so I can hear the waves crashing against the rocks in the evening when the tide is in. Maybe start a little community of people who want to live off the grid. I'll call it Nowhere Bay. It'll be exclusive and hard to find."

"Nowhere Bay?"

"Because it's in the middle of nowhere."

"But if it's full of runaways, you should call it Runaway Bay."

"Runaway Bay. I like it."

"How exclusive will it be?"

"There'll be a gate. And a man who says, 'Who goes there?' when anyone approaches."

"And if it's me?" Denis asked.

"He'll say, 'Welcome home.'"

He could feel Denis' fingers tighten in his hand. Denis said, "I'll run away with you. It sounds blissful."

"Anywhere with you would be bliss."

"I can't tell if you're being cheesy or honest."

"Why can't I be both?"

Denis rolled on top of him, and Oliver could feel his heart beating behind his hoodie. And he felt a stiffness lower down that was not unwelcome.

Oliver tasted Denis' neck, his tongue drawing up from his collarbone to his jawline. "Fate gave you to me," he whispered.

"Fate knows what he's doing," Denis said, kissing Oliver's cheek, his nose, his chin.

Oliver felt the weight of Denis on top of him and he drew his arms around him. His hands caressed him from the neck to the small of his back, his fingers finding the waistband of his boxers and pushing beneath it.

"I'm going to kiss you again," Denis said.

And Oliver said, "Just do it."

Their kiss was more than passion, it was life.

Oliver gripped Denis' body and rolled so that he was on top. His hand slipped down Denis' side and gripped the band of his jeans. He could feel the firmness of him inside.

And, between kisses, Denis said, "Take me."

And from the train, they heard Annabelle call Oliver's name.

"Dammit," Oliver said.

"Shush."

"She needs me."

"She can manage without you for five minutes."

"Ollie? The power is back on," Annabelle shouted.

"The train will leave without us."

"So? Let it."

"You want to get stranded in Boondock Town?"

"We'll put a sign on the edge of the field and call it Runaway Bay."

"Oliver Lloyd," Annabelle shouted. "Get your butt back here at once."

"She needs my butt."

"I need your butt."

"You can have it when she's done with it," Oliver said.

He stood up. "Come on, Mr Rainbow Sparkles. Belfast awaits us." He thrust his hand out and Denis took it. When he was on his feet, Oliver squeezed his fingers and said, "Maybe before we get to Belfast, we'll have nipple sex."

"On a first date? You'll have to buy me dinner first."

They made their way back to the train, picking through the long grasses, and in the silence outside, they heard Mario Lanza singing *O Christmas Tree* from the train's speakers.

Annabelle stood in the doorway above them. "You two look happy."

"Nonsense," Oliver said. He gripped Denis' hand tighter. "We hate each other."

"I can see that. Look at the state of your clothes. That suit's ruined. What were you doing? No. I don't want to know."

Oliver was considering the five-foot climb back into the train carriage when Annabelle's phone rang.

"Hello?" she said.

Oliver turned to Denis and wrapped his arms around his waist. "Let's just walk away, right now; follow the north star until we find the perfect place for Runaway Bay."

"I'm game if you are."

He heard Annabelle say, "This is Annabelle Blake. I handle all of Oliver's calls. Yes, I understand. How bad is it? Yes, I'll tell him."

"Your duty awaits," Denis said.

"Your arms fit around me like no one else has ever done."

"Remember that when whatever celebrity magazine offers to buy your wedding photos."

Annabelle said, "Can't I speak to his doctor? No, I understand. Thank you. I'll pass your message on."

She hung up.

Oliver helped Denis up the five-foot void before climbing in behind him. "What's wrong?" he asked Annabelle.

She seemed reluctant, but she held the phone out to him. "It's Walt. He's been in an accident."

Walt.

Walter fucking Mason.

Of all the times an ex had to come back to haunt him, it had to be now.

"What do you mean, he's been in an accident?"

"I don't know, but it sounds serious."

Oliver looked at Denis, but Denis turned away from him.

He was alone, with his phone in one hand and the rest of his life in another. He wasn't sure which one he'd crush first.

19.

DENIS

When they climbed onto the train, Denis didn't know that his life was about to change again. He wished they hadn't come back—and he knew how selfish that was. Oliver had mentioned Walter when they were lying on the floor of the carriage. He'd called him an ex, but he didn't specify how long ago their relationship ended. Denis assumed it had been years, that Oliver was sober for such a long time. But for all he knew it could have been last month.

"What do you mean, he's been in an accident?" Oliver asked Annabelle. She told him it sounded serious and held the phone towards him. When Oliver took it from her, Denis knew it was probably instinctive—someone hands you something and you take it without thought.

But Denis couldn't look at him when the phone was in his hand. By taking it, he had accepted a piece of his past and brought it into his present.

Denis turned away and stared out the open door at the playground.

When Oliver put his hand on his shoulder, he still couldn't look at him.

"Are you all right?"

He wasn't. "I am."

Oliver kissed his cheek, then he held his thumb on the phone's sensor and redialled the last caller. He paced away from the bar with the phone to one ear and a finger pressed against the other to blot out the sound of the train's Christmas carols.

Denis watched him walk away with a longing he didn't know he could feel.

"They're not answering," Oliver said.

When Adam closed and locked the door to the outside world, Denis felt trapped. At the bar, he studied the fridge of bottled beers and said, "I'll have a stiff glass of iced water, please."

Adam winked. "Good choice."

He settled onto a stool and Annabelle raised her martini glass in salute. The three empty barstools between them felt like a mile.

"Dammit," Oliver said, and he punched redial on the phone screen.

Denis took a drink and wished he'd ordered something stronger. Oliver had already given him his blessing to do so.

"Hello? Hi. Yes. This is Oliver Lloyd. Can you put me through to whichever ward Walter Mason is on? I'm told he was in an accident but that's all I know."

Oliver continued to pace the carriage. When he passed Denis, he brushed his fingers across his back. Denis felt his shoulders stiffen at the touch and he hated himself for physically betraying his emotions.

Oliver waved at Adam to turn the music down. The Christmas carols were annoying, even to Denis whose one wish was to be snowed in on Christmas day with nothing but Oliver and a mug of hot chocolate.

"Hello? I'm sorry, I can't hear you. It's a bad line."

Denis closed his eyes. He pretended he was back in the playground outside, straddling Oliver's hips and free of care. If only Annabelle's phone hadn't rung. Or that Oliver didn't call the hospital back.

But wishful thinking was worse than hindsight.

"Lloyd," Oliver said, slowing his voice and raising his pitch. "Oliver Lloyd."

Heaven was a real place. It was the space between Oliver's arms. It was in the looks they shared on a pair of creaky swings.

And now it was gone.

"Can somebody please tell me what's going on? I'm his what? How can I be his emergency contact?"

Annabelle slipped off her stool and sat beside Denis. She didn't say anything.

She put her hand on top of his.

Denis nodded with a single, slow movement.

"Walt is old news."

"Yeah."

"You and Ollie looked pretty close out there."

"I guess."

"You don't like to talk much, do you?"

"I say what I have to when I need to." He took his hand out from under hers and lifted his glass.

"I must admit," she said, "I didn't like you at first. But you've grown on me."

"How long were they going out?"

"Him and Walt? It was a turbulent eighteen months, I think."

Oliver said, "Say that again. I can't hear you. What time's his surgery?"

"You look upset," Annabelle said.

"I'm not upset."

"Oliver likes you."

"I like him, too."

"So, don't be upset."

"I'm not upset."

He got off his stool. "I'm going to go lie down for a bit." When he closed the door of his cabin, he kicked his bag where it lay on the floor. He still heard Oliver shouting.

"Is it serious? Just tell me, for God's sake."

Oliver's concern for his ex-boyfriend revealed a jealous streak that Denis didn't know he had. But he didn't care to analyse it. Of course he should be concerned about Walter—he may be dying for all Denis knew. But jealousy is an ugly thing that makes you think terrible thoughts.

Denis thought Oliver's intense worry for Walter Mason was a show of his lasting affection. And that meant he had no room in his life for anyone else. Their kiss was not one of longing but of temporary lust.

Denis picked up his backpack. The few things he'd taken out of it, he stuffed back inside, and he left his cabin, pulling the door closed behind him. He slipped across the carriage unnoticed and pushed the door release button.

When he stood in the next carriage, he pulled his hood up, dropped his shoulders, and left without looking behind him.

It was impossible to imagine the night ending any other way. He started it alone, and it would end the same. If the train had been moving, he'd have jumped off the side of it into whatever oblivion awaited him.

He approached one of the exit doors and tried to open it. He needed to get off the train, but the door wouldn't open. His fingers sweated as he pushed the button repeatedly. He could feel a cool breeze from the rubber seal between the two sliding doors, and he realised he couldn't breathe. He had no way out. He was trapped on a train full of people who were staring at him—the guy with Oliver Lloyd a while ago; the one who was mooning over the celebrity like a doting teenage girl.

He couldn't breathe.

He pushed the button.

He couldn't breathe.

He poked his finger at the seal, letting the air in. He could smell the night. And he knew the passengers were watching him, this lunatic at the door. He pressed his mouth against the opening and inhaled, but it was no use. His chest was tight. The whole world was watching him and laughing.

He punched the door with his fist. Breathe, damn it.

He sucked the air through the seal again and filled his lungs. He held it, counted to five, and released his breath. He felt sweat stinging his eyes and he squinted.

He made a fist and dug his fingernails into the palm of his hand. The pain was distracting him from his inability to breathe. And in time, he felt his heart rate come down. He wiped the sweat from his face and stepped away from the door.

Denis passed through a second carriage where little Jamie Collins was asleep in his nammy's arms. She scowled at him as he walked by.

In the next carriage, he looked around for an empty seat and felt a hand on his shoulder. He wished it was Oliver.

When he turned, the drunk woman, Sally, who was no longer so drunk, stared at him. Her mascara had run, and her face was streaked.

"You're not so big," she said.

"Not now. Go peddle your shit somewhere else."

She slapped his face.

Denis walked away from her, found a seat by the window, and threw himself into it. He pressed his forehead against the cool glass and felt his cheek sting. He told himself his eyes were watering from the force of her slap and nothing else.

He clutched his backpack in his lap and could feel a burning heat in his chest. He should have stayed at home. If he hadn't told his mum he was gay, he'd be in his bedroom now, asleep, surrounded by familiar things, not sitting on a train and trying desperately not to cry.

He thought of his dad and tried to conjure up some words of wisdom that might have been said through the years. When he was seven, less than a year before his father took his own life, they were standing in the foyer of the two-screen cinema on the outskirts of Clannon Village, waiting in line to buy tickets to whatever animated kids' movie had come out that summer.

His father had been eating an ice cream they'd bought from a street vendor that Denis no longer wanted, and was trying to find a bin when someone said, "Andy? How's it going?"

Denis watched as his dad shook the man's hand. "Craig. Don't tell me you're here to see a kids' movie."

Craig held up his hand with two tickets in it. "Bruce Willis in Screen Two." He indicated the man standing beside him. "Sorry, this is David. David, this is Andy; we work together."

They shook hands. "Which one of you is the Bruce

Willis fan?" Dad laughed.

"That would be me," David said. "I just love those white vests."

When Denis' mother came out from the girls' toilets with Caroline in her arms and joined them, introductions were repeated, and the same Bruce Willis joke was made.

On their way into the screen, his mum said, "They were nice."

"I've known Craig for years, but I didn't know he was gay."

"How could you not know? You saw how camp he was."

"Really? I never noticed."

"It's hard to miss."

"What if you're not looking for it? Sometimes people are just people, gay or not."

They took their seats and Mum settled Caroline between Denis and Dad. His sister scooped some popcorn into her little hand and spilt most of it on the already sticky floor. "What does gay mean?" she asked.

Mum tried to shush her.

Dad said, "It means you love life."

Dad used to be happy. Denis wondered if his father had ever loved life.

He looked out of the window and could see the children's playground in the distance. If the train didn't start moving soon, he'd go back into the luggage carriage where there were no windows.

He pulled his hood down over his eyes so that he wouldn't have to see the one place he longed to be.

20.

OLIVER

liver couldn't stand still as he held the phone tighter to his ear like it would help improve the terrible signal.

"Just tell me, Doctor. Is he going to survive?"

Walt's doctor wasn't forthcoming with his answers. Over the course of their static-filled conversation, Oliver had pieced together enough words to figure out that he'd been in a drink-driving accident. He couldn't tell if he'd been the driver or a passenger.

It occurred to him that, in all this time, Walt hadn't updated his emergency contact details, though it surprised him that he'd even used Oliver in the first place. Sure, they'd been dating for a while, but Oliver's emergency contact was Annabelle. He'd had no other choice;

his dad was abroad more often than not, and his mother would probably stop for a fresh bottle of gin on her way to visit him in hospital.

He and Walt had never discussed their emergency contacts. They'd never needed to. But of course Walt would use him for that. Not just for his desire for fame, though that was great, but because his dad packed a bag when he was twelve, slammed the door on his way out, and never came back. And although Walt's mother was around, she may as well not have been. She was a crack addict with bad teeth and a nervous tic. She'd asked Oliver for a loan more times than he could count and, though he wanted to believe the money was needed for conventional things, he couldn't bring himself to hand it over. He'd make excuses—forgot to bring his wallet today—and pity her with his smile.

And, back then, he'd head out for the night in Dublin with Walt and get off his face on coke and expensive champagne and forget about Walt's mum. Once, he drank—or choked on—a glass of coke and snorted some champagne with a straw. It gave him a nosebleed and he didn't sleep for three nights.

And even when he was puking for twelve hours, Walt was still offering him more. He had gotten into the dealer's game, too. It's where most of his money came from even as his mother wallowed in her self-imposed poverty. He swore he never supplied her, but Oliver was never certain of that.

"You don't eat where you shit," Walt had said.

"I think the phrase is, 'Don't shit where you eat.'"

"Either way, I'm not putting crap in my mouth, am I?" he said, putting ecstasy in his mouth and leaning forward to kiss Oliver and transfer the high.

Oliver saw the irony now, but at the time he was happy to take the pill and zone out on the dancefloor.

"Are you there? I can't hear you. Will somebody just tell me what's going on?"

Annabelle caught his eye, and he was comforted by her presence. She was always the rock at his side.

The phone crackled and the doctor said, "He's going into surgery now." The words that followed were garbled, but they sounded something like, "Say a prayer."

And if a medical doctor was telling you to pray, you damn well better start praying.

He didn't want him to die. But Walt was an ex. Although the sex was good—or at least good while he rode a high—they'd had their fair share of arguments and fights.

Walt had been a jealous lover. He was always stalking Oliver's Instagram photos, checking who was liking them. It didn't matter that Oliver pointed out he had nothing to do with his Instagram profile—it was managed by Belle. Walt didn't see that. When someone liked more than two or three photos in a row, Walt was all over their profile, calling them out on some perceived flaw. He fat-shamed skinny men, called one guy an ugly runt because he was only five feet three inches, and told a man he was going to come round to his house and smash his windows.

Oliver should have known he was bad news and walked away. But he was high for most of their time together and he was chasing his next fix.

Once, as he was coming down off a serious high, curled up on the floor of his bedroom in a ball, shivering and sweating and hurting, Walt crawled across the floor to him with his phone in his hand. "Who's Anthony Larkin?"

"Who?"

"Anthony Larkin. He's in your DMs with a photo of his junk."

"Set me up a line, will you? I feel like shit."

"Who is he?"

"How should I know? D'you know how many dick pics I get in one week?"

"Are you shagging him?"

"Who?"

"This bloke," Walt said, shoving the phone in Oliver's face.

"Back off, man."

"You're fucking him, aren't you?" Walt pushed him.

"Seriously, Walter. Just put out a line already."

"I'll kill you," Walt said. He punched him on the jaw and again on the nose. Oliver had raised his hands to defend himself, but Walt gripped his wrists and head-butted him.

Oliver had given up. He didn't have the energy to fight back and the pain in his face took away from the gnawing agony in his gut.

When Walt calmed down, his fist soaked in blood from Oliver's nose, he lay on top of him, exhausted.

Oliver fell asleep with Walt lying across him. When he woke, he said, "Are you finished?"

Walt shrugged.

"Put me a line out, will you?"

"Okay."

That was the state of their relationship. They would fight and make up almost daily. But it was mutually beneficial. Walter Mason was getting attention from the press for being in a relationship with Oliver Lloyd, and Oliver was bingeing on tablets, most of which had names he couldn't pronounce.

When he finally sobered up long enough to walk away and check himself into rehab, Oliver was convinced he had gone into The Darlington Manor with a couple of fractured ribs. Walt had beat on him like it was a sport. At the time, he thought he deserved those wounds. But Father Bartosz, with his powerful arms and stronger voice, laid that thought to rest. "No man, no matter how sinful, merits being sinned against. You are more than your needs and better than your desires."

Father Bartosz—Oliver was never sure if that was his first name or last—would bring a fresh bowl of water every day and a cloth. He would say, "Strip to the waist," as he wrung the cloth in the water to bathe his sweating body. Oliver would struggle to pull his T-shirt over his head and Father Bartosz would assist him, with comforting fingers, as though careful not to hurt the broken man whose mind was too fragile a thing to unbalance.

He would make gentle strokes with the damp cloth along Oliver's arms and his chest, wring it again and apply it to his back, and all the while he would be singing a Polish song, a soothing sound that Oliver wished he had recorded so that he could listen to it in times of need.

And he would need it often.

Every evening, Father Bartosz would ask him, "What is your hurt?"

The first few nights, Oliver responded, "Walter Mason."

But soon he realised Walt wasn't the one who was hurting him. When Father Bartosz asked him again, "What is your hurt?" Oliver replied, "I am." And he said the same thing every night, until his final evening in the Manor.

"What is your hurt?" Father Bartosz asked him, standing in his doorway, the cloth floating in his bowl of water.

"Father. I am no longer hurting."

Father Bartosz put his bowl on the bedside table and clapped his hands and cried.

"Why do you cry, Father?"

"Because you are healed."

"You healed me."

"No, child. You healed yourself."

There had been times in the months since then that Oliver wanted to snort a line of coke, drink a bottle of tequila, and go dancing until his feet hurt. But he would look at himself in the mirror and ask, "What is your hurt?"

And he didn't have to answer.

He stared at the phone when the call dropped. Walter Mason was going into surgery, and Oliver wasn't sure how that made him feel. In part, he knew he had brought it on himself. But you can't let go of your past even when you want to. He didn't want his ex-boyfriend to come to any harm, despite not being a nice person.

He looked at Annabelle. Then at Adam.

And he looked around the carriage for Denis.

"Where's he gone?"

"How's Walt?"

"In surgery. I still don't know how bad it is. He was in a car wreck."

"High?"

"Drunk, at least. Who knows with Walter? Where's Denis?"

"He went to his cabin." When Oliver moved in that direction, Annabelle said, "Don't, Ollie. Leave him alone. I think he was pretty upset about the phone call."

"If he's upset, I should talk to him."

"Let him cool off. You just kissed him and then transferred all your attention to your ex-boyfriend."

"That's not what I was doing."

"He knows that. Just let him get his head around it."

Oliver went to his room anyway. He knocked. "Denis? Can I come in?"

Denis didn't answer him.

"I'm coming in, okay?"

When he opened the door, the room was empty. He checked the small bathroom and then he sat on the edge of the bed with his head in his hands. He didn't know how he could have been so foolish. He shouldn't have called the hospital back so urgently. If only he'd explained the situation first.

Denis had left, but he would still be on the train somewhere. Oliver only hoped it wasn't too late.

He went back to Annabelle. "He's gone. I'm going after him."

"Please don't. Let him come back when he's calmed down."

"I can't do that, and you know it."

"Oliver, you two looked pretty intense outside. And then you get this shocking news. His head will be spinning. Let him figure it out himself."

"If it was you, you'd want me coming after you."

"This isn't a fairy tale, Ollie. What are you going to do? Ride through the train on a white horse and swoop him off his feet? He needs to figure his own shit out first."

"Nobody should ever need to figure anything out on their own. You know that. Just look at you and your dad."

Annabelle flattened her lips. He could tell she was biting back a swear word.

"I'm sorry, Belle. But I need to go after him."

"I'm sorry, too. But I honestly think he needs some time alone."

"But I don't want to be alone."

"Are you?"

He nodded. He really was.

He handed the phone back to Annabelle. He straightened his suit jacket, buttoned it, and pushed the release lock to leave the carriage.

21.

DENIS

D enis opened his eyes and realised he'd fallen asleep when the sound of the train's engine penetrated his fugue. A collective cheer rose from the passengers and the public address system chimed.

"Ladies and gentlemen, this is your driver speaking. On behalf of Irish Rail, and all the staff aboard *The Duchess of Dublin*, I wish to offer my sincere apologies for the unexpected delay while we carried out some essential maintenance. I'm pleased to say we are fully operational and will be on our way as soon as we get the green light. Staff will be passing through the train shortly with complimentary drinks. I have been advised that all passengers will receive ten per cent off their next journey onboard any Irish Rail service when they produce their *Duchess of Dublin* ticket at a mainline station. And I'd like to offer my hearty congratulations to Denis Murphy who, I'm told by one of our engineers, is celebrating his ninth birthday today. Congratulations, little man, this song's for you."

Happy Birthday floated out of the speakers.

Denis would murder Tom when he saw him, but he smiled despite his mood.

He sat up in the seat and yawned, shivering as an icy chill stole in from a gap in the window frame where the sealant had worn thin. The flesh on the back of his neck itched as the fine hairs goosed alive. He clutched his backpack and hoped the heating would kick in soon.

The applause redoubled when the train rocked and jolted forward. They were moving.

Denis glanced out of the window in time to see the children's playground move away as though it was a stage piece on a pulley system. Exit stage right.

He pressed his face against the glass so that he could stare at it for as long as possible, and he wished he was back there, in Oliver's arms, carefree. Or careless.

Or both.

But he didn't think Oliver wanted that as much as he did.

Fate has given you to me.

Fate lied.

He came out to two people tonight, and both had rejected him. The backhanded slap from his mother didn't sting as much as Oliver turning away from him for his ex-boyfriend.

His rejection was complete. Nobody wanted him. Not his mother, who wished he was dead. Not Oliver, whose attention was fixed firmly on Walter Mason.

Denis told himself that Oliver had a right to be concerned with Walt's condition, but it stung all the same. He had nothing left. In one night, he'd lost any relationship with his mum, and his heart had been ripped from his chest and crushed underfoot. He'd come home for the Christmas break full of hope; it was his favourite holiday season. And now he was empty. The cloying darkness outside the train hammered at his soul and the sound of the joyous conversations around him was a reminder that he was utterly alone. In a world full of harmony, he was discord. He was a scratch on an otherwise smooth surface.

Denis Murphy wore a smile like most men wear coats. He put it on when he went out, and he took it off at home, and it lay untouched until he needed it again.

Being around people was exhausting. At college, the few close friends he had was often enough stimulus to last him a lifetime that, by the time the weekend came around, he would lock himself in his dorm room, claiming a need to study. But he'd stream reruns of old 90s comedy shows and cry when he should have been laughing.

He hated to admit it—would never say it aloud—but he spent much of his teenage years fighting back tears. Sometimes, when life got too much for him, he would scratch the sharpened point of a pencil across his inner thigh, high enough that no one would see the marks even if he wore shorts, and he'd let the tears roll down his face until his cheeks felt swollen and the tension was gone.

He told himself he wasn't normal. He would look in the mirror and find his flaws—one eye a little bigger than the other, the small scar on his left cheek made by a kitchen knife that Caroline had accidentally thrown at him when she was three. And then he would lie on his bed at night, in the quiet darkness of his teenage isolation, and he would beg his father to come back to him, pray that he would walk through the door and hold him.

And in the morning, he'd put his smile back on and go down for breakfast and his mum would tell him to tuck his school shirt in and straighten his tie. And he'd go through the day, doing all the things that teenage boys do, until he could get home and take off his school uniform as well as his smile.

His only saving grace in high school, apart from Tom's younger brother, Aaron, was a boy named Stephen Jackson who was teased for being overweight even though he was barely larger than anyone else in the class. Denis gravitated towards him for group exercises because sitting beside someone so quiet meant having fewer conversations.

Soon, they were eating lunch together to avoid having to perform the lunchtime ritual of finding a suitable table to sit at. The school cafeteria's seating arrangements were not as defined as the movies would have you believe, but there was a distinct hierarchy. Denis and Stephen sat opposite each other and ate in silence, and when the bell rang, they'd nod and walk back to class without a word.

When they had to do a joint history paper on the Irish War of Independence, Stephen asked Denis to come to his house that weekend to start typing up the report. Clannon Village was a small place, and Stephen lived on a working farm a mile south of the school gates. The farmhouse, huge in comparison to Denis' semi-detached home, was warm when he entered, and dark despite the overhead bulbs that cast orange shadows on the ceilings.

In his bedroom, Stephen typed on his computer while Denis read from a textbook, and later, they lay on the floor beside each other, and Stephen put his hand on Denis' crotch. When Denis didn't object, he pulled the zip down and reached inside. Denis shivered as the excitement buzzed through his body, and he walked home with a genuine smile on his face for the first time in years.

He and Stephen continued to see each other for eight months, and they made a point of appearing neutral at school so as not to arouse suspicion. Denis was happy; he had connected with Stephen on a level deeper than most fourteen-year-olds get to, and he could talk openly and explore his sexuality with a gentle, tender-hearted boy.

Until Stephen's parents got divorced, sold the farmhouse and moved away.

Devastated, Denis couldn't eat for days, despite his mother's protestations. She figured it must have been girl problems and told him it wouldn't be his last heartache, as if that was supposed to cheer him up.

He took to cutting his inner thigh again in the privacy of his bedroom, and for the rest of the school year, he couldn't even bring himself to put the fake smile on his face. He sat in class, alone at a table designed for two, and the 2H pencil at the bottom of his bag called to him. Once, in the bleak darkness of his loneliness a few weeks after Stephen left, he raised his hand in class, asked to go to the bathroom, and he locked himself in the stall. He sharpened the pencil, wood shavings floating to his feet like dying butterflies, and he lowered his trousers and etched the pencil lead into the flesh of his inner thigh where the hairs of adulthood hadn't even reached. He bit his lip to stop from crying out, listening to two boys chat while they pissed, and when he was alone again, he gripped the cuff of his school jumper between his teeth and screamed.

He blotted the blood from his thigh with some toilet paper that he spat on to dampen, and then he wrapped some fresh paper around his leg and pulled his trousers back up. He returned to class and when the maths teacher wrote a formula on the board, he opened his notebook and wrote, *I want to be where my dad is.*

He could feel the blood on his thigh seeping through the toilet paper as though his wound was betraying him.

At fourteen, six years after his father's suicide, Denis

Murphy wanted to join him. The urge to throw himself into the river and sink to the bottom was overpowering. He thought of that caravan holiday at The Downings just before his dad left him forever, and he missed him.

And he missed Stephen.

He punched himself in the stomach every night when he felt like crying because pain was better than tears. And even when he stayed over at Aaron's house and could spend the evening staring at the handsome Tom, he still missed Stephen.

The train rocked as it went around a bend in the track.

He felt more deflated now than he had back then, sitting on the cold train, heading to Belfast with no mum, no dad, no best friend, and no boyfriend. He put his hand on his thigh, remembering the release he used to get from his pencil or the point of a drawing compass. He hadn't done it in years—hadn't wanted to—but the desire to cut himself hit hard.

He didn't have the energy to cry. The tiredness in his eyes came from more than exhaustion. The further away from Clannon Village he got, the lonelier his life had become. He missed Stephen.

He missed Oliver.

Oliver, with his perfect hair and stubbled cheeks, whose eyes would attract magpies with their shine.

Oliver, who wanted someone else.

What was the point?

He wanted to cry.

A nearby passenger said, "This is the best night ever."

And Denis refused to close his eyes because he knew the second he did, the tears would come. He kept them open and stared out the window at his own reflection, a face with one eye bigger than the other and an ugly scar on its cheek the size of a maggot.

He opened his backpack and pushed his hand in among the clothes. At the bottom, he found a pencil and wrapped his fingers around it. He had no privacy; couldn't cut himself here in an open carriage, but holding the pencil was comforting. The lead wasn't sharp enough, anyway. But he was glad that he had it. It was an old friend.

And he had so few of those.

When the door at the head of the carriage opened and a crowd of girls came in, Denis didn't look up. The last thing he needed was the sound of teenagers grating on his nerves.

"Oh my God, it's him," someone whispered loudly. "He's here."

Everyone stood up. And Denis shrank into his seat. The commotion could mean only one thing.

"Denis? Denis, are you here?"

He heard Oliver's voice before he saw him. Surrounded by a gaggle of girls, the celebrity was hard to spot. Denis pulled his hood up and slouched further into his seat but staying put was not an option. Oliver would find him and if he had to look into those eyes again, he would cave in.

He gripped his backpack, made sure Oliver was too

preoccupied with the girls who sought his attention, and he slipped down the carriage to the door. He pushed the button and dashed into the next train car, holding his breath until the door closed.

He couldn't hide forever on a train with no way off until they reached their destination, but he could put off the inevitable for as long as possible.

If he could not look at Oliver, Oliver could not break him.

22.
OLIVER

As he came out of his carriage and into the next, he braced himself for the onslaught of questions and comments. It didn't matter how many times he had to navigate public adoration; it always came as a shock, and after every appearance, he was physically exhausted. It was harder to smile than it was to frown.

Oliver looked around for Denis, hoping no one would notice him, and for a few seconds, he was surrounded only by the noise of quiet conversation. Denis was not in sight and the far end of the carriage felt like a mile away.

"It's Oliver Lloyd," someone said.

Oliver felt every muscle in his body tighten. He smiled, waved, lowered his head, and hoped they wouldn't crowd around him like they always did. Annabelle didn't come with him, still reeling from the visit with her father, and he had no security.

Phone cameras flashed and news of his arrival rippled down the carriage as people stood up to see him.

They touched him like he was a saint bestowing blessings.

"Can I get a selfie, please?"

He posed, smiled, said, "You're welcome," when they thanked him, and he tried to shuffle further down the carriage.

"I'm sorry. Excuse me. Pardon me." He was running out of ways to apologise for pushing past everybody, and he hated that he was the one having to say sorry when they were standing in his way. When somebody bumps into you on the street, they don't say sorry—you do. Like it is always your fault.

Oliver was always at fault. His mother blamed him for his father being abroad too often. His sister blamed him for his mother's drinking. He blamed himself for Walter being a junkie and for Denis running away from him.

"Denis? Are you here?" he called over the tops of heads.

"I love you, Ollie."

"That's very kind, thank you. I'm sorry, can I just squeeze through?"

"Can I get a photo with you?"

"Of course, but I'm kind of in a hurry."

The girl pressed herself against him and held her

phone up to immortalise the moment.

"Thanks," Oliver said, as though it was his privilege to be photographed with a random girl.

He moved forward. Smiled. Nodded. Posed for another selfie.

"Denis? Are you in here?"

The bodies pressed closer, and he found it difficult to walk without butting against someone.

"Denis," he shouted. "Excuse me, please. I need to get through. Denis?"

Bodies crowded him. He had no idea how so many people could fit in one train carriage.

He made it to the narrow end of the car where the cabins were and had to push against the wall to squeeze behind some people.

"Where's that hot P.A. of yours?" some guy asked.

"Denis?" Oliver shouted.

A hand gripped his arm.

Oliver turned with his fist balled. But it was Annabelle's father, Mr Blake. He pulled him into his cabin and closed the door.

"I heard you shouting for ten minutes before you even made it this far."

"Thank you," Oliver said, "but I really need to find someone."

"That lad that was with you? I haven't seen him. Sorry."

Oliver shook his head in dismay. "I should go."

"Can I pour you a drink?"

"I don't drink."

"Mr Lloyd, I—this thing with Annabelle and me. Can I explain?"

"I really don't think it's my place."

"She heard me out, but I need you to understand why I'm here. Why now."

"Mr Blake, please. I can't get involved."

When Mr Blake sat down on the edge of the bed with such abject despondency, Oliver didn't know what to do. He wanted to leave—needed to find Denis—but couldn't walk away from such a saddened face.

He sat on the small desk chair beside the bed.

"She's angry with me, isn't she?"

"I think that's only natural, Mr Blake, given the circumstances."

"Please. Call me Eddie. And I understand her anger, I really do."

"I'm not sure what you want me to say."

"Did she tell you why I'm here?"

"No." It wasn't a lie. After his game of Twister with Denis, when the lights went out and Annabelle joined them at the bar, he spoke to her for a minute. She'd said her dad wanted to mend broken fences, but he didn't ask her what they'd talked about, and she didn't offer.

"Do you remember that shooting in Dublin back in 2001? The lad from Belfast? Of course you don't, you're not old enough." Eddie Blake paused, and Oliver knew not to interrupt his thoughts. "It was pissing down that night. The kind of rain that bounces off the road, it was coming down so hard. I'd been out with a few of the guys from work, celebrating something—probably the fact it was a Wednesday, you know?

"Anyway. We'd been in half a dozen pubs by then. Maybe more. You know what it's like. If only we'd gone to the first pub and stayed there. We'd dash from one pub to the next with our coats up over our heads. Pretty sure we looked like drowned rats by the end of the night."

Oliver surreptitiously checked his watch. The longer he was away from Denis, the worse he felt.

"By about ten o'clock that night, the guys had all gone home, and I was three sheets to the wind and not ready to go anywhere. So, I sat at the bar and ordered another drink, minding my own business.

"I didn't see the door open; didn't know anyone had entered. Next thing I hear is a gunshot. I'll never forget it. Loud as anything. And as I stumble off my stool to the ground, I realise with this level of clarity that I'm spattered in blood—my arms, my shirt, my face.

"I go down. Hard. I thought it was my own blood, I was covered in so much of it. And people are screaming. And running. And I'm crawling under the nearest table. And there's another shot. It's so loud my ears are ringing. There's glass shattering and people screaming and fucked if I know which way is up anymore."

When Eddie looked at him, Oliver could see unshed tears in his eyes.

"I crawl the fuck out of there. Out the back door, along with everyone else. The shooting had stopped.

Bang. And then a pause. And then another bang. And that was it. Someone's dead. Something like that sobers you up, let me tell you. But my head's still ringing and I'm stumbling around outside, going in circles. And the police show up. I was scared. I stood in the shadows and watched as they entered the pub. And then I went home. I had no idea at the time who was shot. Or how many were dead—was it one guy? Was it two? I didn't know.

"I go home. I walked—six miles. I strip my bloodied shirt off and throw it in the bin. And I'm vomiting in the garden when Deirdre, Annabelle's mum, comes out in her dressing gown and smacks me across the back of the head. 'Get the hell inside, you'll wake the neighbours,' she said. And I got the hell inside. I didn't go to work the next day. Or the next. Deirdre thought I was just hungover. She packed Belle off to school and went to work. And when she came home, I was gone."

Eddie fell silent.

Oliver was stunned. But when the quiet itched into an eternity, Oliver said, "Just like that—you got up and left?"

"That's what it looked like, to Belle and her mum. I'm sure they called me a drunken bastard. They had every right. But it wasn't so simple. I didn't leave; I was told to go."

"Told? By who?"

Eddie shrugged. "The IRA? The UVF? Fucked if I know." He took a deep breath before explaining. "While Deirdre and Belle were out that afternoon, there was a knock on the door. I didn't want to answer it, I was still terrified about the shooting two nights before. But they knocked louder and longer. So, I got out of bed where I'd been hiding and opened the door.

"They came in, without an invite. Three men. I'd never seen them before. But one of them pushed me into a chair at the kitchen table and sat a photograph down in front of me. It was a picture of me, standing in the shadows outside the pub, covered in somebody else's blood. By this point, the killing was all over the news. Protestant Belfast lad. Just a young thing. Twenty years old. James Reginald Walker. I'll never forget his name.

"They said they knew I'd shot him twice in the back and when I told them no, it wasn't me, they said, 'When we put your name out, everyone's going to know it was you.' And I said, 'It must be you who did it because it definitely wasn't me.' And they laughed. They just laughed. One of the men—a big, tall fella—he picked up a photo from the top of the fridge and took it out of its frame. It was a picture of Belle and her mum at the beach. And he folded it neatly and put it in his jacket pocket.

"And the guy who'd done all the talking, he said, 'You have six hours. Get out of Ireland. If you come back, we'll kill the girl while your wife watches. And then we'll kill her too.'"

"Jesus," Oliver said.

"Jesus had nothing to do with it, I'll tell you that for free."

"What'd you do?"

"What do you think I did? I packed a bag, took as much money out of our bank account as I needed, and got on a ferry to England."

"You just left your family?"

"I did it to protect them."

"Why didn't you take them with you?"

"That wasn't part of the deal."

Oliver had no words.

"So, there you have it. That's why I left." Tears shed from his eyes and Oliver felt his pain.

"But you're back. Are they in danger? Why are you here?" There was panic in his throat, and he stood. Denis was gone from his mind as Annabelle's safety was in question.

"I have a false passport," Eddie said. "A new name, new life."

"But by being here, you're putting your daughter in danger."

"I'm not staying. I only came to say goodbye."

"Goodbye?"

"Bowel cancer."

Oliver sat down. He puffed up his cheeks before asking, "How long?"

Eddie's smile was curt. "Thanks for being direct. I've got six months. A year if I'm unlucky." He looked at Oliver. "She won't forgive me. Can't you make her see sense?"

"Mr Blake—Eddie—I don't know what to say. Belle's opinion can't be swayed. I wouldn't even try."

"I'm sorry. I shouldn't have asked you. I shouldn't have told you any of this."

"Why did you?"

"I don't expect her to forget the last twenty-odd years. I just want her to know I'm sorry. And I did it to protect her. I didn't want to leave. She was my little girl." He stood up and pointed at the desk behind Oliver. "I wrote her a letter. Would you mind?"

Oliver was hesitant to pick it up. "It's not a suicide note, is it?"

"Maybe it'd be better if it was."

"Don't say that."

"I've arranged a ferry out of Belfast in the morning. I'm going back to London. I'm not going to kill myself; my body's already doing that for me. I'm going to drink port and live out the rest of my days alone. Like I've spent the last twenty years."

Oliver took the letter and slipped it into his pocket.

Eddie Blake offered him his hand.

Oliver pulled him into a hug. "I'll give her the letter as soon as I go back to our carriage."

"No, give it to her after we've arrived in Belfast. I can't suffer another goodbye."

"Do you have treatment? A doctor?"

"Doctors are all miserable, stuffy bastards. I have my diagnosis and I'm living my life the way God intended—fast and loose. Don't feel sorry for me. I have a gorgeous daughter who has a great friend in you."

"What about your wife?"

"Deirdre's better off without me. That was a given from the day we married. They've had good lives. Mine may be over, but theirs doesn't have to be."

At the door, before Eddie opened it to let him leave, Oliver hugged him again, careful not to unbalance him on his walking cane, and he said, "Is there anything I can do?"

"Just give her the letter. And tell her I'm sorry."

"I will."

Back in the carriage, while the passengers were distracted, Oliver slipped down to the door and into the space between cars. Before going into the next carriage, he took a minute for himself to consider how horrible Mr Blake's life had been.

He couldn't imagine the heartache Eddie had suffered, leaving behind his family. Or the pain Annabelle had grown up with.

The world lay heavy at their feet.

Oliver felt emotionally depleted, but he had his own issues to deal with first. He went into the next car.

"Denis?" he called. His voice wasn't that loud, but it attracted enough people near him that he knew he was about to suffer the same fate as before.

"Oh my God, it's Oliver Lloyd."

"Please," he said. He could feel anger rising in his throat. "I'm just looking for my friend. That's all. Nothing more."

"Oh my God, it's him," someone said. "He's here."

And everyone was on their feet. Someone slipped

through the door at the far end of the carriage and Oliver could have sworn it was Denis.

"Denis. Please."

People crowded around him. In a seat nearby, he saw Sally, the drunk who had thrown herself at him.

"Sally? Have you seen Denis?"

She refused to look at him.

"Denis?" he shouted.

Bodies pressed closer.

And he thought about Annabelle. About her father. And about Denis.

"Denis," he cried out.

Someone touched him. "Can I have a selfie?"

Oliver wrapped his arms around himself. He screamed, and as he did, everyone backed away. "Leave me alone. Please. Jesus, I never asked for this. I didn't want any of it. I just want Denis. Leave me alone."

"Ollie?"

He looked up. Denis was there. He pushed through the throng, pulling people out of the way and shouting at them to move. "Get back. He's not cattle; leave him alone." He stood before Oliver, a human barrier.

"Denis." Oliver knew his voice sounded pathetic even as he spoke.

Denis pushed his hood back and his expression was unreadable. "Say what you have to say, Oliver. Say it and let's be done with it. I'm just ready to go home now. And when we get to Belfast, I don't ever want to see you again."

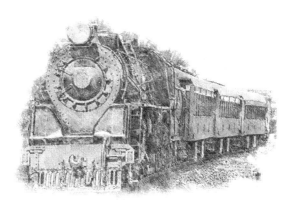

23.

DENIS

D enis stuffed his hands into the pockets of his hoodie. He couldn't read Oliver's facial expression, but he saw the panic that had been rising in him. He recognised it from his own emotions.

He refused to meet Oliver's gaze.

"Will you let me explain?"

"What is there to say?"

Oliver shrugged. "Everything." When Denis nodded, Oliver said, "Not here. Come back to our carriage. Please."

Denis flipped his hood up because he couldn't think of any words that would be appropriate. It was enough of an indication for Oliver to turn and go back to his carriage. *Our* carriage, he'd called it. Denis kept his head down as he walked, refusing to look at anyone, least of all Oliver's back. He heard people calling Oliver's name, asking for selfies, but Oliver didn't stop. They crossed the threshold into the next carriage and the noise was renewed.

"I'm sorry," Oliver said as he pushed through the crowd. Denis heard tears in his voice, but he was certain they wouldn't break free. "Excuse me."

The passengers crowded him. "Ollie. Oliver. Over here, please."

"Let us through."

Oliver was swallowed by the throng and Denis, a few feet behind him, was lost in a sea of bodies. He got on his tiptoes but couldn't see Oliver's head above the others. "Ollie," he shouted. His voice was stolen by the sound of fangirls.

Somebody nudged him. They didn't apologise.

He thrust his elbows out for protection. And then a hand pushed towards him from between two bodies, poking out of the cuff of a blue suit jacket.

Denis gripped the hand and let Oliver pull him through the crowd.

"Back off," someone said. "Give them room, please."

Tom appeared with attitude, pushing back the crowd like a nightclub bouncer. His overalls were dark with oil and grease.

"You lads okay?"

"Can you get us to our carriage?" Oliver asked.

Tom winked at Denis. From his pocket, he took a

small silver whistle, the kind a train conductor would use on the platform, and he blew it. The sound was shrill and piercing and the passengers fell back from him, covering their ears.

"This way, lads," Tom said, and when he marched, the crowd dispersed.

Oliver didn't let go of Denis' hand. They followed Tom through the car and when he pushed the door release button at Oliver's carriage, he gave another toot on his whistle, shook Oliver's hand, and then took Denis by the shoulder as Oliver stepped through the door.

"Are you good?"

"I'm fine. Is this your new profession?"

"I'll never give up working with cars, but trains are my latest secret passion."

"How on earth did you manage to convince the entire staff of a train that you're an engineer?"

"Turns out they use a temp agency for some mechanical assistance. People are always coming and going. Give me another twenty minutes and I'm sure I can convince the driver to let me take the wheel."

"Do trains even have a steering wheel?" Denis asked.

Tom shrugged. "Who's got control of *your* wheel?"

"I do."

"You sure?"

Denis looked through the door that Tom had been holding open, and Oliver was watching them.

"I'm sure."

Tom hugged him, blew his whistle, and marched

away.

Denis followed Oliver into the carriage to the bar and when they got there, Annabelle picked up her drink and said, "Adam, you were going to show me that bottle of 1963 Château Amoureux that you have out the back, weren't you?"

Adam nodded emphatically, and they went into one of the far cabins where the bar's overstock was stored. They closed the door.

"Château Amoureux?" Denis asked Oliver. "Is there really a wine called Castle of Lovers?"

"You speak French?"

"*Je parle un petit peu français. Et toi?*"

"Show off."

Oliver went behind the bar, took a bottle of sparkling water from the small fridge, and twisted the cap off. He reached in for a beer and popped the lid against the wall-mounted bottle opener. He came back around and put the bottles on one of the tables before sitting down and indicating Denis to join him.

For a second, Denis considered the beer, wanted to enjoy the crispness of it, but he picked it up, carried it to the bar, and got a bottle of water.

"You don't have to do that."

"I know." He sat down and forced his gaze to meet Oliver's. He picked at the label on his bottle rather than drinking from it.

"I'm sorry," Oliver said.

Denis nodded.

"I was insensitive. We'd shared a kiss and then literally two seconds later I'm screaming down the phone at a doctor, demanding to know how my ex was doing."

"He was injured. I get it."

"But you don't. You don't get it. Walter is a mess—emotionally. But worse than that, he messed me up. I was addicted, not just to drugs and alcohol but to him, too. I had to be. He was my escape. He had been for eighteen months and even though I knew he was bad for me I couldn't help myself. He was the only thing I had to cling to when my family was combusting around me."

"You still love him?"

"No. I don't think I ever did. But that's not the point. You don't have to love a person to be tied to them. Walt Mason was my lifeline—and yeah, I know how ironic that sounds. He supplied me with all kinds of pills and shit, so much that it could have killed me—and I called him my lifeline. But you don't know what I was going through. That's not an excuse. I did what I did and live with that. But my life was hell, and Walt offered me something no one else could. He gave me release."

Denis shook his head. Everyone had their bad days, him more than most, but he couldn't think what could have been so bad about Oliver's life that he'd call it hell. He was rich and handsome. What more could anyone want?

As if reading his mind, Oliver said, "Not even Annabelle knows this, but my parents are filing for divorce. Dad's been shacked up with his secretary in

Paris for the last two years and he's only come home twice during that time. He thinks we don't know, but the staff do a lot of talking. And my sister is so toxic that her husband doesn't want to be anywhere near her. Shiva is almost five years old, and she sees more of me since she was born than she sees her father. He might as well be dead.

"And in case you haven't noticed, I don't do very well with this celebrity lifestyle. It's not me; I never asked for it. I'm famous because my father is rich, nothing else. At least, that's how it started. Do you know, I was fourteen the first time I got into a nightclub? Fourteen years old and I threatened the doorman with my father's lawyers if he didn't let me in. My face was already splashed across social media, so he knew who I was. And, yeah, I was a brat. If he didn't let me in, I would have called my dad and convinced him to get the bouncer sacked or something. The guy just stamped the back of my hand and let me in.

"God, I got so wasted. But that was me. I was such a little shit and people let me get away with it. Why wouldn't they? Even at fourteen, I had one of Dad's credit cards. I was everybody's best friend."

The train lurched around a bend in the track and the water bottles slid across the table. Denis caught them both. He said nothing, waiting for Oliver to continue.

"A few years later, when I came out, the media made a huge deal over it. Like being gay in the twenty-first century is still a crime. I'm seventeen and my face had become the poster child for homophobes everywhere. There was this rally in Dublin, some anti-gay thing before the same-sex marriage referendum. I'd been in town that afternoon with my mother. We were trying to find a suit for me for Grace's wedding and I swear if I went home with anything but the exact colour she wanted, my sister would have murdered me. I wish she had. We're walking down Grafton Street when we pass the protesters. And what do I see?"

Denis wasn't sure if he had paused for an actual answer, or if he was just formulating his words.

Oliver said, "They had pictures of me on their placards. *God hates fags*, and *Adam and Eve not Adam and Steve*. The usual rhetoric. But here's the worst thing— one of the protesters recognised us and he waved his placard at me and called me a faggot. And there was shit on his placard. Actual human shit smeared across my face on his poster."

"Jeez," Denis said.

Oliver nodded. He didn't speak for a minute. At last, he said, "I'm not trying to say my life was worse than anyone else's by coming out; my mum didn't give a crap who I wanted to kiss. But it was a far more public affair than most. And that public outing made me paranoid. For years I hardly left our home. I'd had a few boyfriends after that, but they never lasted long. They all wanted me for my celebrity status and my parents' money, not for me. And you can always tell when someone is being your friend because they like you, or if it's because they want

227

a holiday on your dad's yacht.

"Anyway, along comes Walter Mason, and he genuinely didn't seem to care who I was. He just wanted to get high. And getting high was something I excelled at. Getting high meant I could forget about my family and my life. When I was off my face, I didn't care that people wanted to smear shit on my photos and use me as an example of all that was unholy."

He took his phone from his pocket and slid it across the table. "If you check my DMs, you'll see half of them are from fans who want to sleep with me, and the other half are from people who use the ugliest language to tell me I'm going to hell for being gay."

Denis didn't touch the phone. He didn't need to.

"So, yeah. I spent my life getting wasted. And Walter Mason was there for me—or at least he was there to supply me, and for a long time, that's all I cared about. I didn't give a damn that he'd beat on me. He'd call me names or blame me when a random guy in a bar tried to chat me up as though it was all my fault. Why would I care about any of that when he was always there to give me my next fix? Walt was my dealer more than my lover. He became my everything, my world. And for every punch he landed on me, he'd make it better with a pill or some speed. I spent my days drunk and my nights in the arms of a dealer. And I had this false happiness, this attitude that if I was too wasted to care about anyone else, nobody else would give a toss about me."

Denis could see the tears in his eyes as he told his

story. He felt the hurt emanating from his pores. He wanted to reach across the table and take his hand, to comfort him, but Oliver's touch felt like a lifetime away.

Before continuing, Oliver scratched the back of his head with a nervousness that belied his stoic tone.

"When Annabelle told me he'd been in an accident, my reaction wasn't one of love. It was confusion. This man from my recent past was hurt and although I didn't want to jump into his arms, I didn't want to see him harmed either. He was a dealer, a violent twat, but he was part of my life. And maybe that makes me a bad person, but I couldn't just turn my back on him when he might have been dying. No one deserves that." He looked up at last and Denis met his gaze. "Do you see now? Do you understand? When that call came through, my brain went into meltdown. I didn't know which way was up. I had you in my arms, and even though I haven't seen Walt in months, there he goes, fucking up my life again by getting himself nearly killed. I hate myself for caring about him. And I hate myself more for letting you slip through my fingers."

For a long time, neither of them spoke. Denis' mind was doing somersaults even more than his stomach was. He never realised how messed up Oliver's life had been. He'd seen a rich kid with rich-kid values, not a broken addict who couldn't escape a miserable existence.

But Oliver had turned his life around. He'd sobered up and it seemed like he cared, as though he knew now what it meant to be a better person.

Denis looked at the door that Annabelle and Adam had disappeared through. He hoped their conversation was less disturbing.

He took a drink from his bottle of water to moisten his dried throat. "You shouldn't hate yourself. I don't."

"You should."

"I'm sorry for reacting the way I did. I jumped to conclusions. We kissed and then your ex pulled you away from me. At least, that's how it felt. You've had a crap life, with shitty friends. And I don't want to be one of those awful people."

"You're not."

"I don't know how you've survived through all that. The fame, the drama. The shit-stained placards. I really like you, Oliver. But I can't do that. I can't be some pin-up model's public boyfriend. I'm not like that."

"I know."

"I couldn't stand the attention."

"I know."

"I would hate to walk down the street and be recognised. You've had to deal with that your whole life—but me, I'd crumble at the first insult. You're strong; stronger than you think. If I had to deal with half of what you've been through, I'd die."

"I know."

Denis twisted his bottle on the table and couldn't meet Oliver's gaze. The sparkling water fizzed, and he wiped his wet fingers on his jeans.

"It's not your fault," he said. "I can't be what you need

me to be."

"I need you to be who you are."

"But I can't handle the celebrity lifestyle. That's not me."

"I know it's not. It's not me, either."

"I wish we were still back at the kids' playground, just you and me. Or better yet, at Runaway Bay. The two of us and a dozen puppies. And no media."

Oliver drummed his knuckles on the table. "So, let's go."

"What?"

"Let's go."

"Where?"

"To Runaway Bay. Why not? We both want it, and I can afford it. A life away from the media. Let's go."

Denis didn't answer him.

"Let's go," Oliver repeated. "Let's go to Runaway Bay."

24.

OLIVER

The silence engulfed him. "Let's go to Runaway Bay," he'd said, as if it was a place that already existed, and he looked at Denis, whose eyes glistened in the dimness of the overhead lighting, whose face was flushed with apparent pain.

And he looked at his lips that were soft and closed and held the promise of a kiss if only he could bring himself to speak the words aloud.

But he didn't speak. And Denis stared at him for an eternity before turning his face to the window, the same window that had revealed to him the children's playground when the train had stopped and gave them the opportunity to share their first kiss under a clear night sky, three days before Christmas.

"Let's go to Runaway Bay," Oliver had said, and he meant it. He would give up everything if only Denis would say yes; if he'd look at him and smile and part his lips not just for a kiss but to say those words that he needed him to say. *Let's go.*

Oliver held his breath. He didn't dare make a sound. He was torn between excitement for a future that didn't involve the paparazzi and celebrity gossip magazines or crushing disappointment at a life without Denis.

He felt the pistons beneath the floor as they spat and sucked, and the train sped up as it approached a hill.

Denis stood, steadied himself against the table as the carriage rocked, and he flattened his lips. Oliver had seen him do it before when he was about to say something weighty.

Oliver got out of his chair and faced him.

"Okay."

"Okay?"

"Yeah. Let's go."

Oliver's breath caught in his chest. He raised his hands but didn't know what to do with them. "Can I hug you?"

"I think you'd better."

"Yeah?"

"Yeah." And Denis came to him. He reached his hands up, cupped Oliver's face, and they kissed.

Panic evaporated from Oliver's body at the same speed as the passion rose. He pulled Denis closer and leaned into the kiss with all his joy. And the sound of the pistons was music beneath his feet.

Denis' lips were his new home. Runaway Bay was in his arms. Wherever they go, Runaway Bay would always be at Denis' side.

Oliver pressed his body tighter against him and remembered the sweet smell of Denis' clean skin from their kiss in the kids' playground. He pushed his fingers through the hair at the back of Denis' head and tasted the sweet poison of his tongue that intoxicated him with desire. When their kiss ended, he nudged his forehead against Denis' and breathed him in.

"I'm serious," he said. "About Runaway Bay."

"Me too."

He laced his fingers with Denis' and tried not to smile at his luck. "I'm not pressuring you into it, am I?"

"Do I look pressured?"

Oliver pulled back to look at him. "Are you happy?"

Denis screwed his face up in thought and shrugged.

"Hey!"

"Of course I'm happy. I like kissing you."

"So, you only want me for my lips?"

"Maybe some other parts, too, but I'm not sure about those yet."

Oliver kissed him again before either of them said anything more. There was a stirring deep in his psyche that he knew had been gnawing at him since they met.

"But definitely these lips," Denis said, leaning back and running his thumb over them, wiping the sheen of kisses from them. "I could get used to these."

"Stop joking around. Is this for real? Are we doing this?"

Denis nodded.

And kissed him again.

And Annabelle and Adam applauded. They had come out of the stock room at last and stood close to each other. Oliver had no idea how long they'd been standing there, but the smile on Belle's face let him know she approved.

Denis blushed and buried his face in Oliver's chest.

The barman and Oliver's P.A., who shared a glance before approaching them, congratulated the couple and hugs were handed out like Christmas presents.

"Are we done with the histrionics now?" Annabelle asked.

"What histrionics?"

She patted them both on the cheek. "I'm talking to the pair of you." She winked at Denis and kissed Oliver's forehead as she ruffled his hair. "I'm going to sit at the bar and drink expensive champagne until it makes me burp. When I turn back around, you boys better not still be standing here."

"What?" Oliver asked, her meaning lost on him.

"Get a room."

"Oh."

And Denis blushed again.

Oliver took his hand and led him to the cabins. He opened the door of Denis' room and closed it behind them. When he leaned against it and shut his eyes, he didn't expect Denis to slip into his arms.

They held each other and kissed.

In time, their kissing eased, and Oliver led Denis to the bed. Denis looked at him, at the bed, and then at the floor.

"I don't mean—I didn't mean that."

"I want to," Denis said. "But not here. Not now."

"Not yet," Oliver agreed. He sat on the edge of the bed and patted the mattress beside him. When Denis joined him, he took his hands. "I'll make some calls in the morning when we finally get off the train. We'll get a house. Someplace in the middle of nowhere. On the coast with plenty of land."

"And a white picket fence?"

"Hell, yeah, a white picket fence. Why not?"

When Denis smiled, Oliver smiled. He couldn't help it.

"Describe it," Denis said.

"It'll be white. And made of pickets."

"The house, not the fence."

They fell into each other's arms and rolled into the small bed. "It'll be big, but not too big. We'll have a piano in the lounge that neither of us can play, so we'll need friends who can gather around it with us and sing Christmas carols—and someone who can actually play it. There'll be a few bedrooms for guests; my niece and your sister—Caroline, isn't it? They can stay with us whenever they want to."

Denis kissed him. "Go on."

Oliver turned onto his back, his arm trapped beneath Denis' neck, and he closed his eyes to visualise it. "It'll be south facing, of course."

"Of course."

"With a view of the ocean. We'll lie awake at night, wrapped in thick blankets and each other's arms, listening to the sound of the crashing waves. And in the morning, you'll make espresso and pancakes and wake me up with breakfast on the porch as we watch the fishing boats weave in and out, casting their nets, not realising that I've already caught the best fish on the menu."

Denis slapped his arm. "Shut up."

"And we'll have a vegetable patch that I tend during the day, and you'll write poetry in the evenings while drinking wine by an open fire."

"Roses are red," Denis recited.

"See? You'll be Poet Laureate in no time."

They kissed, and Oliver held him close. He never wanted to let go. The soft brushed fabric of Denis' hoodie was warm and inviting, and the skin of his neck was sweet.

They fell silent, their faces inches apart, staring at each other as Oliver's fingers trailed down Denis' arm.

"What are you thinking about?" he asked.

Denis' smile was fluid and quick. "How can my life change so fast? Eight hours ago, I was a different person. And then you show up, like a Christmas angel."

"Like Clarence in *It's a Wonderful Life*? The one who

saves George Bailey from drowning by jumping in the water first."

"Oh, my God, I love that movie. And yeah. Exactly like that. You have no idea."

"Every time a bell rings," Oliver said, and Denis recited it with him as he finished the quote with, "an angel gets his wings."

"Attaboy, Clarence," Denis said.

"Is this a thing, now? We're just going to quote movies to each other for the rest of our lives?"

"I think this is the beginning of a beautiful friendship."

"Badges? I don't have to show you any stinking badges."

"I always thought he said 'badgers'," Denis admitted. They laughed.

And they kissed again.

"Seriously, though," Denis said, shuffling down the bed so that he could rest his head on Oliver's chest. "I can't believe how much I've changed in one night."

"Of all the trains in all the world, you had to sneak onto mine."

Denis slapped him and laughed. "I'm being serious."

"So am I. You could have got on any train in any direction. But you got on this one with me."

"Fate," Denis said.

"Right?" Oliver agreed.

"I can hear your heartbeat."

"Is it skipping?"

"Corny. No. It's saying, *Den—is; Den—is; Den—is*."

"It knows what I want."

When Annabelle's soft knuckles rapped at the door, Oliver felt Denis stiffen as though the interruption was unwelcome.

"What is it?" Oliver called.

She didn't open the door. "I've had a voicemail from the hospital."

Denis rolled off him and sat up, and Oliver flipped his legs over the side to join him. They looked at each other.

Denis nodded.

Oliver ran his hand over his chin. He had trimmed his stubble that morning but already he could feel it growing out. He took Denis' hands in his and kept his gaze locked on his gleaming eyes. "Go on," he called.

There was a pause. Then Annabelle said, "He's out of surgery. He's going to be okay. Sorry to disturb you, I just thought you'd want to know."

Oliver lowered his face to Denis' shoulder. His limbs were numb, and he realised after she had spoken that he'd been holding his breath. He couldn't speak.

"Thanks," he heard Denis say. "Thanks for letting us know." Denis wrapped his arms around him and he felt at home, as though he belonged there.

Annabelle's shadow moved away from the door.

Denis kissed the top of his head. "Are you all right?"

Oliver nodded.

"You sure?"

He straightened up, kissed Denis, and said, "I didn't

want to see him hurt, but you know I have no feelings for him like that. He's out of my life. He might be a lying, cheating scumbag, but no one deserves to suffer. I don't want him to have any power over us. His name shouldn't be something we fear."

Denis touched his cheek. "We're made up of snippets from our past, a cocktail of memories. But memories are just that—the past. You have a future now."

"You're my future."

"Maybe you'll regret that one day, too."

"Never."

"I hope not."

Oliver pulled Denis down onto the bed and kissed him. "Stop being a pessimist."

"I can't help it. It's who I am."

He cuddled into him. "I'll teach you."

"You're hardly the world's most famous optimist."

"Then we'll teach each other. You're in for the ride of your life."

"It can't be any longer than this train ride," Denis said.

And they laughed.

25.

DENIS

The rocking motion of the train lulled Denis to sleep in Oliver's arms and when he woke, he was still smiling. They were spooning on top of the small bed, their shoes discarded in the corner of the room, and Denis' hoodie was twisted around him and riding up at the front.

He yawned and turned to face Oliver and saw that he was sleeping. He didn't dare breathe in case he woke him. He stared at Oliver's face, those lips that he had kissed, the strong cheekbones and the dark eyelashes that fluttered in a dream.

He couldn't believe how much his life had changed in a matter of hours. Last night, he'd stood on a bridge overlooking Broad Meadow River, and he gave serious consideration to diving into the icy waters and never coming up. Now, he just wanted to dive into Oliver's arms and stay there forever.

Runaway Bay. It sounded like a dream, and he didn't know if it was really going to happen or if it was just the wishful thinking of a young man who hated his celebrity life, or who needed a break from the world. Either way, Denis would be there as long as he needed him.

Oliver's arm was draped over his side and Denis nudged closer. He reached up and held his fingers above the softness of Oliver's cheek, not touching, just feeling the heat of his skin.

He wanted to kiss him, to wake him up and feel the press of Oliver's lips kissing him back. But he also wanted to stare at his sleeping face for as long as he could. There was a nervous anxiety in the pit of his stomach that wasn't fear. It was warmer than that.

Through the wide window above his head, Denis could see the thin silver clouds easing between the dim stars, and he couldn't tell what time it was, but he knew the sky was brightening in the east.

Oliver twitched in his sleep and pulled Denis tighter. Their noses met.

Without opening his eyes, Oliver said, "Hi."

"Oh. Hey."

"Were you staring at me?"

"Maybe."

Oliver tilted his face, his eyes still closed, and kissed him.

Denis felt the electricity of desire charging the atoms of his existence.

"I dreamt I met this really cute boy," Oliver said.

"Oh, yeah?"

Oliver opened his eyes. "Oh, look; it wasn't a dream."

"Shut up."

They kissed again, and Denis allowed the gentle swaying of the train to rock them together. He brushed Oliver's fringe off his forehead, and he kissed him there.

When Oliver's hand touched his arm, he said, "I want your hoodie. It's so soft."

"It was a Christmas present from my mum. You can have it." He turned around again so that they were spooning, with Oliver's chest pressed against his back.

"She really hurt you, didn't she?"

"Hurt me? She disowned me."

"Will you talk to her? I'm sure she was just shocked."

"She said she wished I was dead."

"She didn't mean it."

"She sounded like she meant it."

Denis was glad to be facing away from Oliver. He didn't want him to see the tears that filled his eyes.

"She's your mum. She'll come around. Has she ever given you any anti-gay vibes before?"

"No. But I hadn't come out before."

"Promise me you'll talk to her. Tell her how you feel."

"I don't think I want to see her ever again."

"You'll have to when you go to pick up your clothes and bring them to Runaway Bay."

Denis let the tears out without sobbing. He just released them, and they left him. "I promise."

And Oliver kissed the back of his neck.

When the public address system chimed, neither of them moved. "Ladies and gentlemen, this is your driver speaking. It's December twenty-third and the time is approaching six-thirty. You'll be pleased to know we'll be arriving at Belfast's Great Victoria Street Station in just over twenty minutes. Great Victoria Street Station is our final destination. Irish Rail apologises once again for the delays to your journey, and we wish you a very happy Christmas and a pleasant and prosperous New Year."

Denis heard the cheers erupting through the train. A journey that should have taken less than seven hours, lasted more than ten. No wonder the passengers were delighted.

"They weren't counting on a breakdown on their first journey," Oliver said. "I'm pretty sure *The Duchess of Dublin* is going to be retired before the end of the day. It'll be a PR nightmare."

"But it wasn't a nightmare, was it?"

"Not for me."

They kissed. And Oliver held him for a few minutes before Annabelle knocked on the door.

"Up and at 'em," she called. "I hope you remember whose boxers are whose."

Oliver reached over the edge of the bed, picked up a shoe, and threw it at the door. They heard her laughing as she walked away.

"Do we really have to get up?" Denis asked. "Can't we tell the driver not to stop?"

"What happens when the track runs out?"

"We can Thelma-and-Louise our way off the cliffs."

"In a steam train? Sounds fun." Oliver sat up, dragging his arm out from under Denis' waist. "Come on, lazybones."

Denis pulled him back down. "Don't go."

"You drive me insane."

"That's my plan."

"Fine. Two more minutes."

When they did get up and Denis packed his things back into his bag, he checked his phone. There was a text from Caroline that she'd sent late last night. *Mum's gone to bed at last. Come home, Denny. She'll calm down, I know she will.*

Standing at the bar, Adam poured coffee into souvenir *Duchess of Dublin* travel mugs and passed them out. "I know it hasn't been an entirely fun night, but it's been a pleasure serving you all."

Annabelle said, "When we get to Belfast, what're your plans for breakfast? I don't fancy eating alone and I know these two are going to want to disappear somewhere quiet together."

"Hey," Oliver objected. But he took Denis' hand and smiled.

"She's right," Denis said.

Adam adjusted the bowtie at his neck and said, "Well,

I would never abandon a damsel in distress."

"It's a date," Annabelle said.

Denis and Oliver stood by the window, watching Belfast roll by as the train inched towards its destination. The sky was brighter now but still dark this close to Christmas. At least it wasn't raining.

"I've never been to Belfast before."

Denis looked at him. "Never? I've been here a couple of times, but I was just a kid. Dad brought me when I was five."

"We should go exploring before heading back to Dublin."

They held each other as the train eased into Great Victoria Street Station. The brakes screeched and the smoke from the engine's chimney swirled a muddy pool across the windows. There was only one news crew on the platform that Denis could see when the train came to a stop and the smoke cleared.

"If there were others, they must have given up when we didn't arrive during the night as scheduled," Oliver said.

"Will you have to do an interview?"

"They'll be expecting it, but I don't want to."

"We're really doing this Runaway Bay thing, right?" When Oliver nodded, Denis said, "Then this can be your last ever interview. Your swansong before you disappear into the sunset."

"And spend the rest of my days in bed with you?"

"That's what I'm counting on."

Oliver kissed him, and Denis picked up his backpack. They waited as the other passengers got off the train and hurried out of the platform. In the open doorway, Oliver pulled Denis into his arms. "My last interview," he said.

"Your last one ever."

"You'll wait for me?"

"Of course. Good luck."

He watched Oliver step off the train and walk towards the camera crew. Behind him, Annabelle and Adam approached. He had untied his bowtie and Annabelle was wearing his jacket.

She studied Denis in the doorway. "Are you worth it?"

He shrugged. "No."

"Good answer. Maybe you are." She kissed his cheek, and when he gave her a questioning look, she pointed above his head. In the doorway, taped to the ceiling, was a sprig of artificial mistletoe.

Adam shook his hand. "I like you, but not enough to kiss you."

"Shaking hands under the mistletoe is a far nicer tradition."

"Best of luck."

Annabelle said, "I'll text Ollie once we've had breakfast. Don't break his heart."

"I won't."

He watched them walk away, and then he stepped off the train. The platform was almost empty, passengers pushed out by burly security guards and held back from the exits for Oliver Lloyd's safety. There were a few stragglers as well as Oliver and the news crew. The air was cold, and he breathed in the smell of coal smoke and diesel fumes.

At the far side of the train, towards the back, he watched the last few passengers alighting. He saw Tom, who waved at him. He had his arm wrapped around a girl's shoulders, and Denis recognised her as the girl who'd been forced the wear a dress and suggested that he come back to her cabin not long after he got on the train.

Tom spoke to the girl whose name Denis didn't know, and then he jogged up the platform to him.

They high-fived because shaking hands was too grown up a thing to do with the boy you'd been crushing on for years, and embracing was too intimate under the circumstances.

Tom had changed out of the overalls, but his face and hands were still smeared with grease. "You look happy."

"I am," Denis said. "Looks like sneaking on a train to find a girl worked for you, then?"

"I only met her an hour ago, but yeah. She seems nice. Too bad her parents are right behind her."

"So, you're done being a train engineer?"

"It was fun while it lasted. Think I'll try for a pilot's role next time."

"Lock up your daughters, Tom is taking to the skies."

They sat on one of the benches along the platform and Denis watched Oliver talking to the news crew. He couldn't hear what he was saying.

Tom nudged him. "Are you happy you came?"

"Yeah."

"Oliver Lloyd, eh? What's that like?"

"I don't know yet. I like him. And I think he likes me."

"That was obvious from the minute I saw you two together."

"Do I really make my feelings so obvious?"

"Don't knock it," Tom said. "Being an open book is better than being closed off." He paused, leaning forward on the bench to rest his elbows on his knees. "So. No more funny business?"

"Funny business?"

"You know what I mean. Back in Clannon Village. On the bridge."

"I don't know what you're talking about," Denis said, and he blushed.

"I might come across as stupid sometimes, but I'm not thick."

"I think you're the smartest man I know."

"Well, the smartest man you know knew there was something up on the bridge. You weren't just passing the time."

"No."

"Why were you even thinking of doing something so terrible?"

"I was going through some stuff."

"But you're feeling better now, right?"

Denis leaned forward to match Tom's posture, and he glanced at Oliver. "Yeah. I'm over it. I was having a bad night."

"We all have bad nights. You just have to make it to the dawn and things don't seem so bad." He stood. "You still have my number, don't you? Call me. Any time. If you need to talk. Or if Oliver Lloyd pisses you off. I'll punch him for you."

"I will. Now, go; your date is waiting for you, Tom."

Tom pulled him in for a hug. "I ain't joking. You call me. For any reason. Even if you just want to tell me how good Oliver Lloyd looks naked."

"Oh, my God. Do you ever shut up?" Denis laughed.

They hugged again, and he watched Tom walk away. When he passed the camera crew, he stopped, interrupted Oliver's interview, and slapped him on the back.

Denis didn't know what he said, but Oliver looked behind him and waved. His face was blushing fire, and the cameraman couldn't hold the camera still he was laughing so hard.

Denis groaned, and he waited for the interview to wrap up and the crew to leave.

When they left the station ten minutes later, Oliver draped his arm over Denis' shoulder, and they passed a charity Santa ringing his bell in the street. Oliver stopped, pulled out his wallet, and dropped two fifty-Euro notes into Santa's bucket.

"I fancy pancakes," he said, taking Denis' hand.

"There's a great place right on the corner of Hope

Street," Santa said. "Tell them I sent you."

"Hope Street. That sounds like a good sign. Thanks, Santa."

"Merry Christmas, lads."

They found the place and settled into a booth while the waitress poured coffee and took their order. They stared out the window as Belfast woke up and commuters made their way to work, and Oliver said they were the best pancakes he'd ever had.

Annabelle sent him a text to let him know where she was, and Oliver said he'd call her later. "We should go exploring. Let's see the sights."

"What did Tom say to you when you were being interviewed?" Denis asked.

"He told me to call him when I find out what you look like naked."

"He said the same to me."

Before they left the café, Oliver said, "I'll make some calls when I get home. About finding a suitable location for Runaway Bay. Will you do me a favour?"

"Anything."

"Go home. Talk to your mum. Just talk to her. Then you can come and spend Christmas at mine if you need to. My mum won't care, and you can meet Shiva. It's her birthday soon."

"I'm not sure Mum will want to talk. That's a big ask."

"I know it is." He reached across the table and took Denis' hands. "She's had the night to get over her initial shock. If she doesn't come around to the idea, I'm here for you. She may need more time, but you should at least give her the chance."

Denis gazed into Oliver's eyes. "I'm scared."

"I've got you."

"If you don't let go of my hands, I'm going to fall for you."

"If I do let go, I'll float away. Talk to her."

"Okay," Denis said. And Oliver leaned across the table and kissed him.

26.

DENIS & OLIVER

When the taxi pulled up outside his house, Denis couldn't get out of the car. He stared at the semi-detached home with his forehead pressed against the window. The driver gave him a minute before saying, "This is it, right?"

Denis paid the fare and stood on the street. Just a few short steps and he'd be at the garden gate, but his feet were glued to the pavement.

When the front door opened, Caroline waved at him. She met him halfway down the garden path as he came through the gate, and she threw herself into his arms. It pushed him off balance and he stumbled back, dropping his rucksack. "Woah, I was only gone for one night. You don't hug me this hard when I've been away at uni for months."

She squeezed him tighter, and he carried her into the house. Closing the door, he whispered, "Where's Mum?"

"In her room."

"How is she today?"

"She's barely said anything, but she hasn't been screaming or crying."

Denis looked up the dark stairs and felt his mother's despair leaking down through the ceiling. "I should go up and see her."

"Want me to come with you?"

"No. I need to do this on my own."

He put his foot on the bottom stair and held the banister. He didn't want to climb any further. He looked back at Caroline and her smile was weak, her arms wrapped around herself in a comforting hug. "I've got a joke for you," he said, taking two more stairs.

"Yeah?"

"Did you know scientists have found the main cause of homosexuality?"

"What is it?"

"It's the Large Hard-on Collider."

Caroline put her finger in her mouth, pretending to retch, and Denis steeled his nerves. He climbed the stairs.

His mother's bedroom door was closed, and he remembered the last time he'd stood outside it, close to tears, knowing she was upset on the other side of the door. Although he wished his dad had never been taken from him, he wanted to be eight years old again, with no care in the world.

But the past is gone. It can never be recaptured.

He knocked, but she didn't answer.

"Mum?"

Denis opened the door and found the room in darkness. It was two-thirty in the afternoon and still light outside, but she had drawn the curtains. In her doorway, Denis stared at her back as she sat on the edge of the bed, in the same place she'd been when he'd discovered her there the day after his dad's funeral.

"Mum?"

Scrunched tissues were strewn across the bed beside her and discarded at her feet. Caroline said she hadn't been crying, but he could see that she was.

"Can we talk?"

She didn't look at him. "Can you please ask Caroline to run to the supermarket? We'll need something for dinner."

"She can go in a minute. Can we talk first?"

He heard her sigh, and it was the only indication that she would allow him to speak. She didn't nod her head or shrug. She just sighed.

Denis came around the bed and saw that she was wearing one bedroom slipper; the other had been kicked off and lay on its side. At least she had changed out of yesterday's clothes.

He sat down, sinking into the soft mattress at the end of the bed, separated from her by a mountain of tissues and grief. His mum pulled another tissue from the box on her nightstand and balled it in her fist as though she was preparing herself for more tears.

"I'm sorry," he said. She didn't respond. "I don't know what else to say."

His mum tore at the tissue in her hands with an absent mind. "When you were three years old, and I was seven months pregnant with Caroline, your dad and I took you shopping in Dublin. You were at that age when you didn't want to sit in a pushchair and needed to walk everywhere. Your dad had to stoop just to hold your hand, and you were going so slow, gawking at every shop window, dragging your feet when we tried to pick up the pace.

"My back was sore from being upright for too long and Dad suggested we sit on one of the benches in the square and wait while he got ice creams. There was this street artist, one of those men that stand like a statue until you put money in their hat, and then they start to move. You screamed to go up to him and I was in so much pain, I swear if my waters broke there and then on the street I wouldn't have cared. So, I gave you fifty cents and let you go to him. It wasn't far; I could see you. I didn't think I was doing anything wrong. You put the coin in his hat and off he moved. Oh my God, you could giggle for Ireland."

Denis looked away from her. He couldn't stand seeing the pain in her face.

"But then a crowd gathered around him, watching

his little dance, and I lost sight of you. It was just for a second. I forced myself off that bench and I pushed my way through the crowd. And there you were, in this statue's arms, still laughing even as he handed you back to me. Just a second. You were out of sight for such a short space of time, and yet the eternity that existed there, the lifetime of misery I felt crashing down on me if I had lost you—mothers don't spend their lives worrying about all the things that might happen; we grieve all the things that could happen as if they already did. In that second, I had lost my baby, my sweet baby boy. And I still carry that pain with me today."

"Mum." He had no other words.

"When your father came back, he handed you the biggest ice cream cone I'd ever seen, and he sat beside me on the bench as you ran in circles around us. He'd bought me mint choc-chip because he knew it was the only ice cream I craved during pregnancy, and he put his hand on mine. It's like he could sense the panic I'd been feeling without me saying anything. Your dad was like that. He was always the calm one, the rational one. Not like me."

Denis said, "I'm sorry for all the hurt I've ever given you."

"It's not your place to say sorry. You're my child. You will always be my little boy. Your dad, in all his wisdom, taught me that we are responsible for our actions, not our feelings. Sometimes we can't help our feelings, but when we understand that we can correct them. I had forgotten. I'm sorry for forcing my feelings on you before I had a chance to correct them."

"It's okay."

"No. It will never be okay. I hurt you. I kicked you out of the house and I swore I would never be one of those mothers." She turned to him and took his hands. Denis held her gaze through his tears. "I hate my reaction. I hate that I hurt you. I'm not saying it's going to be easy, but I want us to get over this. Are you sure about—? I mean, can you change?"

"Mother."

"Okay. Let's get through this. Can we do that?"

"Can you accept that I'm gay?"

"Can you accept that I'll try?"

"I can do that."

"Okay."

Denis shuffled closer and she held him in her arms as she used to when he was a child. He sobbed against her shoulder, and she cried into his hair. She rocked him in their shared grief. Their relationship was changed forever—as all things must change.

He'd had a long time to get used to being gay; his mother had had only one night. In time, he hoped, she would not only get used to it but embrace it, understand him.

"Your dad would get it," she said, clinging to him.

"Would he?"

"He'd be cracking jokes by now and asking to meet your boyfriend." She straightened up, kissed his forehead, and opened the curtains, casting light on their tiny existence. "Do you have one?"

"A boyfriend? Kind of. I guess so. Yeah. Yes, I do."

"I'm glad. I would hate for you to be alone."

"You should have a boyfriend, too. It's about time."

"I don't think I need another Gregg in my life, do you?"

"It doesn't have to be someone like Gregg," Denis said, remembering the guy who had told him off at church for jiggling his leg. "You could find someone more like Dad."

"That would be impossible. No one is like your dad."

Later, when Caroline had walked down to the supermarket and used her staff discount to buy some frozen pizzas, Mum cooked them in the oven and served them on the dining room table.

Denis called Oliver, who answered on the first ring. "How did it go?"

"Better than I hoped," he said, closing his bedroom door for some privacy. "She's slowly coming around to the idea."

"But she's not angry with you anymore?"

"No."

"See? I told you it would work itself out."

"I miss you."

"It's only been four hours."

"What? You don't miss me too?"

"Of course I do," Oliver said. "I want to kiss you."

When he hung up the phone and joined his mum and

sister in the dining room, Caroline put some Christmas carols on, and they ate pizza and forgot about their worries. They watched *It's a Wonderful Life*, and Denis thought about Oliver near the end when George Bailey looked to the heavens and said, "Attaboy, Clarence."

Caroline was asleep on the sofa and his mum was crying, though he was sure it wasn't just because of the movie.

They celebrated Christmas as a family, and Denis spent as much time as he could with Oliver but kept him away from home—it was too soon.

Ten days later he returned to Dublin for university.

Before he left, his mum handed him an envelope—as she always did—and said, "It's not much, but maybe it'll pay for some new textbooks or whatever you need." She paused as Caroline walked past them, carrying Denis' bags out to the waiting taxi, and when they were alone again, she said, "I've been looking online. At some support groups."

"Mum. You don't have to do anything you're not comfortable with."

"No, I want to. I need to. There are none in Clannon Village, surprise, surprise. But I found one for parents of LGBTQ children in Dublin, right near your campus. I thought maybe if I come down one evening, we could get dinner?"

"I'd love that. And well done for getting the letters in order."

"Did I say it right? LGBTQ? I practised all morning."

He laughed and they hugged.

And as he rode the taxi to the train station, he smiled.

When he got back to his dorm later that night, his phone pinged.

What time's your first class tomorrow?

Denis called him. "I don't have to go in until noon. Why?"

"Look outside."

"Why?"

"Just do it."

Denis walked to the window and flicked the blinds apart. "If you're standing outside my window like a stalker, I'm going to call campus security."

He heard the sparkle of Oliver's laughter. "I'm not. Just look outside."

In the street below, a black limo was parked across from his building. The driver stood by the rear door, holding it open.

"Get in the car."

"Because that's not creepy," Denis joked. "Why don't you just come up."

"I'm not in the car, dummy."

"Where are you?"

"That's a surprise. I'll see you soon." Oliver hung up.

Denis waved at the driver that he'd be a few minutes, and he packed some clothes in a bag. He didn't know if he was going for an overnight stay, but he wasn't taking any chances. When he got downstairs, he said, "Where are we going? Oliver didn't specify."

"Mr Lloyd expressly forbade me from answering that question, Mr Murphy."

"You can call me Denis."

"Yes, sir, Mr Murphy."

Denis got in the limo and saw a bottle of champagne chilling in an ice bucket. The note taped to the side of it said, *Don't drink too much. See you in a couple of hours.*

"Hours?" Denis said out loud. "Where are we going?"

"Can't say, sir."

A little after ten o'clock that night, the car pulled down a dirt road, its headlights illuminating the twisting path. Denis could smell the ocean even with the windows closed. He saw a wooden sign swinging on a rope chain across the road that said, *Lahaine Beach. Closed for winter.*

The car stopped and the driver got out. When he opened the door for Denis, he said, "This is as far as I can take you. Just hop over the chain and follow the path down the hill. Here's a flashlight."

Wary, Denis used the torch to guide his descent. As he went over a hill, he saw a stunning, V-shaped beach beneath him, and a solitary house nestled among the hills above it, with its lights on, inviting him closer.

He walked towards it, and when he was close enough, he heard music coming from the open door. And Oliver was there, wearing a pair of jeans and a fitted T-shirt despite the freezing temperatures. He held a single red rose in his hands.

"What is this?"

"That's how you're going to greet me? Not even a kiss?"

They kissed, and Denis tasted the memory of all their previous kisses in it. "I've missed you."

"I missed you, too. Come inside."

In the small home, an open fire burned, and there was a thick rug in front of it and a bottle of sparkling water with two glasses.

Oliver filled them and handed one to Denis. "Well? What do you think?"

"Think of what?"

"Runaway Bay."

"For real?"

They kissed again, and Oliver led him to the bedroom.

"Aren't you going to give me a tour?"

"Later."

"Okay." And he let himself be swept through the house and into a warmth that caught in his chest to match the nervous butterflies in his stomach.

Oliver held him, and they fell to the bed together, a jumble of limbs and kisses. And as the night blanched towards the dawn, they explored their relationship in ways Denis had longed for since that night on the train. He tasted him and, when he did, he tasted God.

The sound of the crashing waves woke him in the morning as the sun was coming up. Denis stared at Oliver's sleeping face, unable to keep from smiling, and then he rolled out of bed. He took a spare blanket from the wardrobe, wrapped it around himself, and went to the kitchen to make coffee. With a warming mug in hand, he went to the front door and opened it, standing in the cold breeze, staring down at the beach below. The tide was in, and he let the steam from his coffee warm his face.

Runaway Bay. He had made it.

"It'll be amazing in the summer," Oliver said from behind him. When Denis turned, he saw him standing there in his boxers, hugging himself for warmth. "Got some room under that blanket?"

Denis opened the blanket and let him in. And together they watched the waves batter the sandy rocks below.

"We'll build other houses," Oliver said. "Make a little community of people like us. People who want a quiet life."

"That's amazing. But what about your family, your duties in the public eye?"

"I'm not in the public eye anymore. I never wanted it to begin with. Now it's just me and you."

"Are you sure?"

Oliver pulled him closer. "I've never been more certain in my life."

The sun broke through the clouds and dazzled the waves, and a lonely seagull cried out to the horizon as it circled the grey sky above them.

And Denis smiled.

He was home.

Simon Doyle
RUNAWAY RIDGE

RUNAWAY BAY BOOK 2

COMING SOON

Find out more at

www.simondoylebooks.com

About Simon Doyle

Simon Doyle (he/him) was born and raised Ireland. He discovered that he could travel the world on a shoestring by reading books at a very young age. When he won a local poetry competition at the age of nine, it sparked a lifetime love of words. But he swears never to write poetry again.

His first novel release is *Runaway Train*, book 1 of the Runaway Bay series.

He lives with three cats, two dogs, and Lucas, his human soulmate. They met in kindergarten. Where all good stories begin.

Find Simon online at www.simondoylebooks.com.

Printed in Great Britain
by Amazon